"One of the great series in the history of the American detective story!"
—*The New York Times*

"[Spenser is] the sassiest, funniest, most-enjoyable-to-read-about private eye around today."
—*The Cincinnati Post*

"Spenser novels are addictive."
—*The Denver Post*

"They just don't make private eyes tougher or funnier. The dialogue sparkles."
—*People*

"Robert B. Parker has taken his place beside Dashiell Hammett, Raymond Chandler, and Ross Macdonald."
—*The Boston Globe*

"Spenser probably had more to do with changing the private eye from a coffin-chaser to a full-bodied human being than any other detective hero."
—*Chicago Sun-Times*

"Parker is now the best writer of this kind of fiction in business today."
—*The New Republic*

"The toughest, funniest, wisest private eye in the field these days."
—*The Houston Post*

Books by Robert B. Parker from Dell

THE
JUDAS GOAT

Robert B. Parker

A DELL / SEYMOUR LAWRENCE BOOK

Published by
Dell Publishing
a division of
Random House, Inc.
1540 Broadway
New York, New York 10036

If you purchased this book without a cover you should be aware that this book
is stolen property. It was reported as "unsold and destroyed" to the publisher
and neither the author nor the publisher has received any payment for this
"stripped book."

Copyright © 1978 by Robert B. Parker

All rights reserved. No part of this book may be reproduced or transmitted in
any form or by any means, electronic or mechanical, including photo-
copying, recording, or by any information storage and retrieval system,
without the written permission of the Publisher, except where permitted by
law. For information address: Delacorte Press/Seymour Lawrence, New
York, New York.

The trademark Dell® is registered in the U.S. Patent and
Trademark Office.

ISBN: 0-440-14196-6

Reprinted by arrangement with Delacorte Press/Seymour Lawrence

Printed in the United States of America

One Previous Dell Edition

August 1987

OPM   30   29   28

1

Hugh Dixon's home sat on a hill in Weston and looked out over the low Massachusetts hills as if asphalt had not been invented yet. It was a big fieldstone house that looked like it ought to have vineyards, and the front entrance was porticoed. It didn't look like the kind of place where they have much truck with private cops, but you can't judge a house by its portico. I parked in the lower parking lot as befitted my social status and climbed the winding drive to the house. Birds sang. Somewhere out of sight on the grounds I could hear a hedge being clipped. The bell made the standard high-tone chime sound in the house when I pushed the button, and while I waited for a servant to let me in I checked my appearance reflected in the full-length windows on each side of the door. There was no way to tell, looking at me, that I only had $387 in the bank. Three-piece white linen suit, blue striped shirt, white silk tie and mahogany loafers with understated tassels that Gucci would have sold his soul for. Maybe Dixon could hire me to stand around and dress up the place. As long as I kept my coat buttoned you couldn't see the gun.

The servant who answered was Asian and male. He wore a white coat and black trousers. I gave him my card and he let me stand in the foyer while he went and showed it to someone. The floor of the foyer was polished stone, and opened into a two-storied entry room with a balcony running around the second story and white plaster frieze around the ceiling. A grand piano sat in the middle of the room and an oil portrait of a stern person was on the wall over a sideboard.

The servant returned and I followed him through the house and out onto the terrace. A man with a huge torso was sitting in a wheel chair with a light gray blanket over his lap and legs. He had a big head and thick black hair with a lot of gray and no sideburns. His face was thick-featured with a big meaty nose and long earlobes. The servant said, "Mr. Dixon," and gestured me toward him. Dixon didn't move as I walked over to him. He stared out over the hills. There was no sign of a book or magazine. No indication of paperwork, portable radio, TV, just the hills to look at. In his lap was a yellow cat, asleep. There was nothing else on the terrace. No other furniture, not even a chair for me.

From this side of the house I couldn't hear the clippers anymore.

I said, "Mr. Dixon?"

He turned, just his head, the rest of him motionless, and looked at me.

"I'm Spenser," I said. "You wanted to talk to me about doing some work for you."

Full front, his face was accurate enough. It looked the way a face should, but it was like a skillful and uninspired sculpture. There was no motion in the face. No sense that blood flowed beneath it and thoughts evolved behind it. It was all surface, exact, detailed and dead.

Except the eyes. The eyes snarled with life and purpose, or something like that. I didn't know exactly what then. Now I do.

I stood. He looked. The cat slept. "How good are you, Spenser?"

"Depends on what you want me to be good at."

"How good are you at doing what you're told?"

"Mediocre," I said. "That's one reason I didn't last with the cops."

"How good are you at hanging in there when it's tough?"

"On a scale of ten, ten."

"If I hire you on for something will you quit in the middle?"

"Maybe. If, for instance, you bullshitted me when we started and I got in and found out I'd been bullshitted. I might pack it in on you."

"What will you do for twenty thousand dollars?"

"What are we going to do, Mr. Dixon, play twenty questions until I guess what you want to hire me for?"

"How much you think I weigh?" Dixon said.

"Two forty-five, two fifty," I said. "But I can't see under the blanket."

"I weigh one hundred eighty. My legs are like two strings on a balloon."

I didn't say anything.

He took an 8x10 matted photograph out from under the blanket and held it out to me. The cat awoke and jumped down, annoyed. I took the picture. It was a Bachrach photo of a handsome fortyish woman and two well-bred-looking girls in their late teens. Vassar maybe, or Smith. I started to hand it back to him. He shook his head, left once, right once. "No," he said, "you keep it."

"Your family?"

"Used to be, they got blown into hamburg by a bomb in

a restaurant in London a year ago. I remember my daughter's left foot was on the floor next to me, not attached to the rest of her, just her foot, with her cork-soled shoe still on. I'd bought her the shoe that morning.''

"I'm sorry" didn't have the right ring for a moment like that so I didn't try. I said, "That how you ended up in the chair?"

He nodded once down, once up. "I was in the hospital for nearly a year.''

His voice was like his face, flat and accurate and unhuman. There was a stillness in him that only his eyes denied.

"And I got something to do with this.''

He nodded again. Once up, once down. "I want them found.''

"The bombers?''

Nod.

"You know who they are?''

"No. The London police say it's probably a group called Liberty.''

"Why would they blow you up?''

"Because we were where they threw the bomb. They did not know us, or care about us. They had other things to think about and they blew my entire family into garbage. I want them found.''

"And that's all you know?''

"I know what they look like. I was awake through it all, and I lay there and looked at each of them and memorized their faces. I'd know every one of them the minute I saw them. That's all I could do. I was paralyzed and I couldn't move and I looked at them as they stood in the rubble and looked at what they'd done, and I memorized everything about them.''

He took a manila folder out from under the blanket and gave it to me. "A Scotland Yard detective and an artist came with one of those drawing packs while I was in the hospital and we made these pictures and I gave them the descriptions."

In the folder were nine Identikit sketches of young people, eight men and a woman, and ten pages of typewritten descriptions.

"I had copies made," he said. "The pictures are pretty good. All of them."

"Do I keep these too?" I said.

"Yes."

"You want me to find these people?"

"Yes. I'll give you twenty-five hundred dollars a head, twenty-five thousand for the lot. And expenses."

"Dead or alive?"

"Either one."

"I don't do assassinations."

"I'm not asking you to do assassinations. But if you have to kill one or all of them, you still get paid. Either way. I just want them caught."

"And what?"

"And whatever you do with murderers. Brought to justice, punished. Jailed. Executed. That's not your problem. I want them found."

"Where do I start looking?"

"I don't know. I know what I've told you. I suppose you should start in London. That's where they killed us."

I don't think the pronoun was a mistake. He was mostly dead too.

"Okay. I'll need some money."

From his shirt pocket he took a card and held it out to me. I took it and read it. It said, "Jason Carroll,

Attorney at Law." Classy. No address, just the name and title.

"He's at One Hundred Federal Street," Dixon said. "Go there and tell him how much you need."

"If I'm going to London I'll need a lot."

"Doesn't matter. You say. When can you go?"

"Fortunately I'm between cases," I said. "I can leave tomorrow."

He said, "I had you checked out. You're between cases a lot. Twenty thousand dollars is the biggest money you've ever seen. You've been minor league all your life."

"Why waste all that bread on a minor leaguer then?"

"Because you're the best I could get. You're tough, you won't cheat me, you'll stick. I heard that from my people. I also heard that sometimes you think you're Captain Midnight. Mostly that's why you stayed in the minors, I heard. For me that's good. A hungry Captain Midnight is just what I need."

"Sometimes I think I'm Hop Harrigan," I said.

"No matter. If I could do this myself I would. But I can't. So I've got to hire you."

"And sometimes you think you're Daddy Warbucks. Just so it's all straight between us. I'll find these people for you. I'm not only the best you can get. I'm the best there is. But the things I won't do for money are one hell of a lot more numerous than the things I will do."

"Good. A little ego doesn't hurt. I don't care what you do or what your philosophy of life is or whether you're good or bad or if you wet the bed at night. All I care about is these nine people. I want them. Twenty-five hundred a head. Dead or alive. The ones you get alive I want to see. The ones you get dead, I want proof."

"Okay," I said. He didn't offer to shake hands. I didn't

offer to salute. He was staring out at the hills again. The cat jumped back up in his lap. "And you want me to keep the picture of your family?" I said.

He didn't look at me. "Yes. Look at it every morning when you get up and remember that the people you're after blew them into mincemeat."

I nodded. He didn't see me. I don't think he saw anything. He looked at the hills. The cat was already asleep again in his lap. I found my way out.

2

The secretary in Jason Carroll's outer office had blond hair that looked real and a tan that looked all over. I speculated on the all-overness as she led me down the hall to Carroll. She was wearing a blue top and tight white pants.

Carroll got up from behind his chrome and onyx desk and came around to greet me. He was blond too, and tan, and slim in a double-breasted blue blazer and white trousers. They looked like a dance team. Sissy and Bobby.

"Glad to see you, Spenser. Come in. Sit down. Mr. Dixon told me you'd be stopping by." He had a firm and practiced handshake, and a Princeton class ring. I sat on a chrome couch with black leather cushions, near a picture window from which you could see a lot of the harbor and some of the railroad yards behind what was left of South Station. A stereo was playing something classical very softly.

"My office is on the second floor over a cigar store," I said.

"Do you like it there?" Carroll asked.

"It's closer to sea level," I said. "This is a little rarified for me."

There were oil paintings of horses on the office walls.

"Would you care for a drink," Carroll said.

"Beer would be good," I said.

"Would Coors be all right? I bring it back whenever I'm out west."

"Yeah, okay. Coors is okay for a domestic beer, I guess."

"I can give you Heineken's if you prefer. Light or dark."

"I'm kidding, Mr. Carroll, Coors would be swell. I can't usually tell one beer from another. As long as it's cold."

He touched an intercom switch and said, "Jan, could we have two Coors please." Then he leaned back in his high leather swivel chair, and folded his hands over his stomach and said, "How can I help?"

The blonde came in with two cans of beer and two chilled glasses on a small tray. She served me first, probably my Jack Nicholson smile, then her boss, and went out.

"Hugh Dixon has hired me to go to London and start looking for the people who killed his wife and daughters. I'll need five grand to start with and he said you'd give me what I need."

"Of course." He took a checkbook from the middle drawer of his desk and wrote a check.

"Will this be enough?"

"For now. If I want more will you send it?"

"As much as you need."

I drank a little Coors from the can. Rocky Mountain spring water. Zowie.

"Tell me a little about Hugh Dixon," I said.

"His financial position is extremely stable," Carroll said. "He has a great many financial interests all over the world. All of which he has acquired through his own efforts. He is a truly self-made man."

"I figured he could pay his bills. I was more interested in what kind of man he is."

"Very successful. Very successful. A real genius for business and finance. I don't think he had a great deal of formal education. I think he started as a cement finisher or something. Then he got a truck and then a backhoe, and by the time he was twenty-five he was on his way."

Carroll wasn't going to talk about Dixon, I guessed. He was just going to talk about his money.

"How did he make most of it? What sort of business?"

If you can't lick 'em, join 'em.

"Building trades at first, and then trucking, and now he has conglomerated so extensively that one cannot specify his business anymore."

"Those are tough trades," I said. "Candy asses do not flourish there."

Carroll looked a little pained. "Certainly not," he said. "Mr. Dixon is a very strong and resourceful man." Carroll sipped a little of his beer. He used the glass. His nails were manicured. His movements were languid and elegant. Breeding, I thought. Ivy League will do that for you. Probably went to Choate too.

"The terrible tragedy of his family . . ." Carroll couldn't find the words for a minute and settled for shaking his head. "They said he shouldn't be alive either. His injuries were so terrible. He should have died. It's miraculous, the doctors said."

"I think he had something to do," I said. "I think he wouldn't die because he had to get even."

"And for that he's hired you."

"Yeah."

"I will help all I can. I went to London when it . . . when he was injured. I know the police on the case and so forth. I can put you in touch with someone in Mr. Dixon's London office who can help on the scene. I handle all of

Mr. Dixon's affairs. Or at least many of them. Especially since the accident."

"Okay," I said. "Do this for me. Give me the name of the person who runs the office over there. Have them get me a hotel room. I'll fly over tonight."

"Do you have a passport?" Carroll looked doubtful.

"Yeah."

"I'll have Jan put you on a flight for London. Do you have a preference?"

"I don't care for biplanes."

"No, I suppose not. If it doesn't matter I'll have Jan arrange for flight fifty-five, Pan Am, leaves every night for London at eight. First class all right?"

"That'll be fine. How do you know there will be room?"

"Mr. Dixon's organization flies extensively. We have a somewhat special status with the airlines."

"I'll bet you do."

"Mr. Michael Flanders will meet you at Heathrow Airport tomorrow morning. He's from Mr. Dixon's London office and will be able to fill you in."

"I imagine you have a somewhat special status with Mr. Flanders."

"Why do you say so?"

"How do you know he'll be free tomorrow morning?"

"Oh, I see. Yes. Well, everyone in the organization knows how strongly Mr. Dixon feels about this business and everyone is ready to do anything necessary."

I finished my beer. Carroll took another sip of his. A man who sips beer is not trustworthy. He smiled at me, white teeth in perfect order, looked at his watch, two hands, nothing so gauche as a digital, and said, "Nearly noon. I expect you'll have some packing to do."

"Yeah. And maybe a few phone calls to the State Department and such."

He raised his eyebrows.

"I'm not going over to look at the *Beowulf* manuscript in the British Museum. I gotta bring a gun. I need to know the rules on that."

"Oh, of course, I really don't know anything about that sort of thing."

"Yeah, that's why I'm going and you're not."

He flashed his perfect caps at me again. "The tickets will be at the Pan Am counter at Logan," he said. "I hope you have a good trip. And . . . I don't quite know what one says at such a time. Good hunting, I suppose, but that sounds awfully dramatic."

"Except when Trevor Howard says it," I said.

On the way out I gave Jan the thumbs-up gesture like in the old RAF movies. I think she was offended.

3

My first move was to call the airline. They said I could bring a handgun as long as it was disassembled, packed in a suitcase and checked through. The ammunition had to be separate. Of course it couldn't be carried aboard.

"Okay if I chew gum when my ears pop?" I said.

"Certainly, sir."

"Thank you."

Next I called the British Consulate. They told me that if I were bringing in a shotgun there would be no problem. I could simply carry it in. No papers required.

"I had in mind a thirty-eight caliber Smith and Wesson revolver. A shotgun in a hip holster tends to chafe. And carrying it around London at high port seems a bit showy."

"Indeed. Well, for a handgun the regulations state that if you are properly licensed it will be held at customs until you have received authorization from the chief of police in the city or town of your visit. In this case, you say London?"

"Yes."

"Well, that is where you should apply. It is not permitted of course to bring in machine guns, submachine guns, automatic rifles or any weapon capable of firing a gas-disseminating missile."

"Oh, damn," I said.

Then I called Carroll back. "Have your man in London arrange a permit for me with the London cops." I gave him the serial number, the number of my Mass carry license and the number of my private detective license.

"They may be sticky about issuing this without your presence."

"If they are they are. I'll be there in the morning. Maybe Flanders can have softened them up at least. Don't you people have a somewhat special status with the London fuzz?"

"We will do what we can, Mr. Spenser," he said, and hung up.

A little abrupt for a guy with his breeding. I looked at my watch: 2:00. I looked out my office window. On Mass Avenue a thin old man with a goatee was walking a small old dog on a leash. Even from two stories up you could see the leash was new. Bright metal links and a red leather handle. The old man paused and rummaged through a little basket that was attached to a lamppost. The dog sat in that still patient way old dogs have, his short legs a little bowed.

I called Susan Silverman. She wasn't home. I called my answering service. There were no messages. I told them I was out of town on business. Didn't know when I'd be back. The girl at the other end took the news without a quiver.

I locked up the office and went home to pack. A suitcase, a flight bag and a garment bag for my other suit. I packed two boxes of .38 bullets in the suitcase. Took the cylinder out of the gun and packed it in two pieces in the flight bag along with the holster. By three-fifteen I was packed. I called Susan Silverman again. No answer.

There are people in the city of Boston who have threatened to kill me. I don't like to walk around without a gun.

So I took my spare, and stuck it in my belt at the small of my back. It was a Colt .357 Magnum with a four-inch barrel. I kept it around in case I was ever attacked by a finback whale, and it was heavy and uncomfortable under my coat as I took Carroll's check down to my bank and cashed it.

"Would you like this in traveler's checks, Mr. Spenser?"

"No. Plain money. If you have any English money I'd take that."

"I'm sorry. We could get you some perhaps Friday."

"No. Just give me the greenies. I'll change it over there."

"Are you sure you want to walk around with this amount in cash?"

"Yes. Look at my boyish face. Would someone mug me?"

"Well, you're quite a big man."

"But oh so gentle," I said.

Back in my apartment at quarter to four I called Susan Silverman again. No answer.

I got out the phone book and called the registrar's office at the Harvard Summer School.

"I'm trying to locate a student. Mrs. Silverman. She's taking a couple of courses there in counseling, I think."

There was some discussion of how difficult it would be to find a student like that without more information. They'd transfer me to the School of Education.

The School of Education offices were closing at four-thirty and it would be quite difficult to locate a student. Had I tried the registrar? Yes, I had. Perhaps someone in the Department of Counseling and Guidance could help me. She switched me there. Did I know the professor's name. No, I didn't. The course number? No. Well, it would be very difficult.

"Not as difficult as I will be if I have to come over there and kick a professor."

"I beg your pardon?"

"Just check the schedules. Tell me if there's a counseling course meeting at this hour or later. You must have schedules. Pretend this isn't a matter of life and death. Pretend I have a government grant to award. Pretend I'm Solomon Guggenheim."

"I believe that Solomon Guggenheim is dead," she said.

"Jesus Christ . . ."

"But I'll check," she said. "Hold the line, please." There was distant typing and vague movement at the other end of the line and in thirty seconds the secretary came back on.

"There's a class in Techniques of Counseling, Professor More, that meets from two-o-five to four fifty-five."

"Where is it?"

She told me. I hung up and headed for Harvard Square. It was four-twenty.

At four-forty I found a hydrant on Mass Avenue outside the Harvard Yard and parked in front of it. You could usually count on a hydrant. I asked a young woman in tennis shorts and hiking boots to direct me to Sever Hall and at four-fifty-six was waiting under a tree near the steps when Susan came out. She was wearing a blue madras jumpsuit with a big gold zipper, and carrying her books in a huge white canvas shoulder bag. She had a quality coming down the steps that she always had. She looked as if it were her building and she was strolling out to survey the grounds. I felt the jolt. I'd been looking at her for about three years now but every time I saw her I felt a kind of jolt, a body shock that was tangible. It made the muscles in my neck and shoulders tighten. She saw me and her face brightened and she smiled.

Two undergraduates eyed her covertly. The jumpsuit fitted her well. Her dark hair glistened in the sunshine and as she got close I could see my reflection in the opaque lenses of her big sunglasses. My white three-piece suit looked terrific.

She said to me, "I beg your pardon, are you a Greek multibillionaire shipping magnate and member of the international jet set?"

I said, "Yes, I am, would you care to marry me and live on my private island in great luxury?"

She said, "Yes, I would, but I'm committed to a small-time thug in Boston and first I'll have to shake him."

"It's not the thug I mind," I said. "It's the small-time."

She hooked her arm through mine and said, "You're big-time with me, kid."

As we walked through the Yard several students and faculty eyed Susan. I didn't blame them but looked hard at them anyway. It's good to keep in practice.

"Why are you here?" she said.

"I gotta go to England at eight tonight and I wanted some time to say goodbye."

"How long?"

"I don't know. Could be long. Could be some months. I can't tell."

"I will miss you," she said.

"We'll miss each other."

"Yes."

"I'm parked out on Mass Avenue."

"I parked at Everett Station and took the subway in. We can go to your apartment and I'll drive you to the airport in your car."

"Okay," I said. "But don't be so bossy. You know how I hate a bossy broad."

"Bossy?"

"Yeah."

"Did you have a plan for our farewell celebration?"

"Yeah."

"Forget it."

"Okay, boss."

She squeezed my arm and smiled. It was a stunner of a smile. There was something in it. Mischief was too weak a word. Evil too strong. But it was always there in the smile. Something that seemed to be saying, *You know what would be fun to do?*

I held the door for her and as she slid into my car the jumpsuit stretched tight and smooth over her thigh. I went around and got in and started the car.

"It strikes me," I said, "that if you were wearing underwear beneath that jumpsuit it would show. It doesn't show."

"That's for me to know and you to find out, big fella."

"Oh, good," I said, "the celebration is back on."

4

I found out about the underwear, and some other things. Most of the other things I already knew, but it was a pleasure to be reminded. Afterward we lay on top of my bed, with the afternoon sun shining in. Her body, strong, and a little damp from mutual exertion, glistened where the sun touched it.

"You are a strong and active person," I said.

"Regular exercise," she said. "And a positive attitude."

"I think you wrinkled my white linen suit."

"It would have wrinkled on the airplane anyway."

We got dressed and walked up Boylston Street and across the Prudential Center to a restaurant called St. Botolph. It was one of the zillion California-theme restaurants that had appeared in the wake of urban renewal like dandelions on a new seeded lawn. Tucked back of the Colonnade Hotel, it was brick and had hanging plants and relative informality where one could actually get a good meat loaf. Among other things.

I had the meat loaf and Susan had scallops Provençale. There wasn't much to say. I told her about the job.

"Bounty hunter," she said.

"Yeah, I guess so. Just like the movies."

"Do you have a plan?"

Her make-up was expert. Eye liner, eye shadow, color

on the cheekbones, lipstick. She probably looked better at forty than she had at twenty. There were small lines at the corners of her eyes, and smile suggestions at the edges of her mouth that added to her face, gave it pattern and meaning.

"Same old plan I always have. I'll show up and mess around and see if I can get something stirring and see what happens. Maybe put an ad in the papers offering a big reward."

"A group like that? Do you think a reward could get one of them to turn another in?"

I shrugged. "Maybe. Maybe it would get them to make contact with me. One way or another. I have to have a contact. I need a Judas goat."

"Might they try to kill you if they know you're there?"

"Maybe. I plan to thwart them."

"And then you'll have your contact," Susan said.

"Yeah."

She shook her head. "This will not be a pleasant time for me."

"I know . . . I won't like it that much either."

"Maybe part of you won't. But you're having a grand adventure too. Tom Swift, Bounty Hunter. Part of you will have a wonderful time."

"That was truer before I knew you," I said. "Even bounty hunting is less fun without you."

"I think that's true. I appreciate it. I know that you are what you are. But if I lose you it will be chronic. It will be something I'll never completely get over."

"I'll come back," I said. "I won't die away from you."

"Oh, Jesus," she said, and her voice filled. She turned her head away.

My throat was very tight and my eyes burned. "I know

the feeling," I said. "If I weren't such a tough manly bastard, I might come very close to sniffling a little myself."

She turned back toward me. Her eyes were very shiny, but her face was smooth and she said, "Well, maybe you, cupcake, but not me. I'm going to do one excerpt from my famous Miss Kitty impression and then we are going to laugh and chatter brightly till flight time." She put her hand on my forearm, and looked at me hard and leaned forward and said, "Be careful, Matt."

"A man's gotta do what he's gotta do, Kitty," I said. "Let's have a beer."

We were chatty and bright for the rest of the meal and the ride to the airport. Susan dropped me off at the International Terminal. I got out, unlocked the trunk, took out my luggage, put the .357 in the trunk, locked it and leaned into the car.

"I won't go in with you," she said. "Sitting and waiting in airports is too dismal. Send me a postcard. I'll be here when you come back."

I kissed her goodbye and hauled my luggage into the terminal.

The tickets were at the Pan Am desk as promised. I picked them up, checked my luggage through and went up to wait at the loading gate. It was a slow night at the International Terminal. I cleared the security check, found a seat near the boarding ramp and got out my book. I was working on a scholarly book that year. *Regeneration Through Violence*, by a guy named Richard Slotkin. A friend of Susan's had lent it to me to read because he wanted what he called "an untutored reaction from someone in the field." He was an English teacher at Tufts and could be excused that kind of talk. More or less.

I liked the book but I couldn't concentrate. Sitting alone at night in an airport is a lonely feeling. And waiting to fly away to another country, by yourself, on a nearly empty plane was very lonely. I half decided to turn around and call Susan and say come get me. I minded being alone more as I got older. Or was it just Susan. Either way. Ten years ago this would have been a great adventure. Now I wanted to run.

At eight-thirty we boarded. At eight-fifty we took off. By nine-fifteen I had my first beer from the stewardess and a bag of Smokehouse Almonds. I began to feel better. Tomorrow perhaps I could have dinner in Simpson's and maybe for lunch I could find a nice Indian restaurant. By ten I had drunk three beers and eaten perhaps half a pound of almonds. The flight was not crowded and the steward-ess was attentive. Probably drawn by the elegance of my three-piece linen suit. Even wrinkled.

I read my book and ignored the movie and listened to the oldies but goodies channel on the headphones and had a few more beers, and my mood brightened some more. After midnight I stretched out across several seats and took a nap. When I woke up the stewardesses were serving coffee and rolls and the sun was shining in the windows.

We landed at Heathrow Airport outside of London at ten-fifty-five London time and I stumbled off the plane, stiff from sleeping on the seats. The coffee and rolls were sloshing around with the beer and Smokehouse Almonds.

For simple hodgepodge confusion and complicated extent, Heathrow Airport's name leads all the rest. I followed arrows and took Bus A and followed more arrows and finally found myself in the line at the passport window. The clerk looked at my passport, smiled and said, "Nice to see you, Mr. Spenser. Would you please step over to the security office, there."

"They've reported me. I'm to be arrested for excessive beer consumption on an international flight."

The clerk smiled and nodded toward the security office. "Right over there, please, sir."

I took my passport and went to the office. Inside was a security officer in uniform and a tall thin man, with long teeth, smoking a cigarette and wearing a dark green shirt with a brown tie.

"My name is Spenser," I said. "People at the passport desk sent me over."

The tall thin guy said, "Welcome to England, Spenser. I'm Michael Flanders."

We shook hands.

"Do you have baggage checks?"

I did.

"Let me have them, will you. I'll have your baggage taken care of."

He gave the checks to the security man, and steered me out of the office with his hand on my elbow. We came out a different door and I realized we'd cleared customs. Flanders reached inside his tweed jacket and brought out an envelope with my name on it.

"Here," he said. "I was able to arrange this with the authorities this morning."

I opened the envelope. It was a gun permit.

"Not bad," I said.

We came out of the terminal building underneath one of the walkways that connects the second floors of everything at Heathrow. A black London cab was there and a porter was loading my luggage in while the security man watched.

"Not bad," I said.

Flanders smiled. "Nothing, really. Mr. Dixon's name has considerable sway here as it does in so many places." He gestured me into the cab, the driver came around and said something I didn't understand and we started off.

Flanders said to the cabbie, "Mayfair Hotel, if you

would.'' And leaned back and lit another cigarette. His fingers were long and bony and stained with nicotine.

"We're putting you up in the Mayfair," he said to me. "It's a first-rate hotel and nicely located. I hope it will be satisfactory."

"Last case I was on," I said, "I slept two nights in a rented Pinto. I can make do okay in the Mayfair."

"Well, good," he said.

"You know why I'm here," I said.

"I do."

"What can you tell me?"

"Not very much, I'm afraid. Perhaps when we get you settled we can have lunch and talk about it. I imagine you'd like to freshen up a bit, get that suit off to the dry cleaners."

"Sure wrinkles on an airplane, doesn't it?"

"Indeed."

5

The Mayfair was a big flossy-looking hotel near Berkeley Square. Flanders paid the cabbie, turned the bags over to the hall porter and steered me to the desk. He didn't seem to have a lot of confidence in me. A hired thug from the provinces, can barely speak the language, no doubt. I checked my heel for a cow flap.

My room had a bed, a bureau, a blue wing chair, a small mahogany table and a white tiled bathroom. The window looked out over an airshaft into the building next door. Old-world charm. Flanders tipped the bell man, and checked his watch.

"One o'clock," he said. "Perhaps you'd like to take the afternoon and get settled, then we could have dinner and I could tell you what I know. Do you need money?"

"I have money, but I need pounds," I said.

"Yes," he said. "Of course. I'll have it changed for you." He took a big wallet from inside his jacket pocket. "Here's one hundred pounds," he said, "should you need it to hold you over."

"Thanks." I took my wallet out of my left hip pocket, and dug out $2500. "If you could change that for me, I'd appreciate it. Take out the hundred."

He looked at my wallet with some distaste. It was fat and slovenly.

"No need," he said. "Mr. Dixon's money, you know. He's been quite explicit about treating you well."

"So far so good," I said. "I won't tell him you got me a room on an airshaft."

"I am sorry about that," Flanders said. "It's peak season for touists, you know, and the notice was short."

"My lips are sealed," I said.

Flanders smiled tentatively. He wasn't sure if he was being kidded.

"Shall I come by for you, say six?"

"Six is good, but why not meet somewhere. I can find my way. If I get lost I'll ask a cop."

"Very well, would you care to try Simpson's-on-the-Strand? It's rather a London institution."

"Good, see you there at six-fifteen."

He gave me the address and departed. I unpacked and reassembled my gun, loaded it and put it on the night table.

Then I shaved, brushed my teeth and took a shower. I picked up the phone and asked the front desk to call me at five-thirty. Then I took a nap on the top of the spread. I missed Susan.

At five-forty-five, vigorous and alert, with a spring in my step and my revolver back in its hip holster, I strode out the main entrance of the Mayfair. I turned down Berkeley Street and headed for Piccadilly.

I had a city map that I'd bought in a shop in the hotel, and I'd been in London once before a few years back, before Susan, when I'd come for a week with Brenda Loring. I walked down Piccadilly, stopped at Fortnum and Mason and looked at the package food stuffs in the window. I was excited. I like cities and London was a city the way New York is a city. The fun it would be to stroll around Fortnum and Mason with Susan and buy some smoked quail's eggs or a jellied game hen or something imported from the Khyber Pass.

I moved on up into Piccadilly Circus, which was implacably ordinary, movie theaters and fast foods, turned right on Haymarket and walked on down to Trafalgar Square, Nelson and the lions, and the National Gallery and the goddamned pigeons. Kids were in competition to see who could accumulate the most pigeons on and around them. Walking up the Strand I passed a London cop walking peaceably along, hands behind his back, walkie-talkie in his hip pocket, the mike pinned to his lapel. His nightstick was artfully concealed in a deep and inconspicuous pocket.

As I walked I could feel an excited tight feeling in my stomach. I kept thinking of Samuel Johnson, and Shakespeare. "The old country," I thought. Which wasn't quite so. My family was Irish. But it was the ancestral home, anyway, for people who spoke English and could read it.

Simpson's was on the right, just past the Savoy Hotel. I wondered if they played "Stompin' at the Savoy" over the music in the elevators. Probably the wrong Savoy. I turned into Simpson's, which was oak paneled and high ceilinged, and spoke to the maître d'. The maître d' assigned a subordinate to take me to Flanders, who rose as I approached. So did the man with him. Very classy.

"Mr. Spenser, Inspector Downes, of the police. I asked him to join us, if that's all right with you."

I wondered what happened if it weren't all right. Did Downes back away out of the restaurant, bowing apologetically?

"Fine with me," I said. We shook hands. The waiter pulled out my chair. We sat down.

"A drink?" Flanders said.

"Draught beer," I said.

"Whiskey," Downes said.

Flanders ordered Kir.

"Inspector Downes worked on the Dixon case," Flanders said, "and is a specialist in this kind of urban guerrilla crime that we see so much of these days."

Downes smiled modestly. "I'm not sure expert is appropriate, but I've dealt with a good many, you know."

The waiter returned with the drinks. The beer was cold, at least, but much flatter than American beer. I drank some. Flanders sipped at his Kir. Downes had his whiskey straight without ice or water, in a small tumbler, and sipped it like a cordial. He was fair-skinned with a big round face and shiny pink cheekbones. His body under the black civil-servicey-looking suit was heavy and sort of slack. Not fat, just quite relaxed. There was a sense of slow power about him.

"Oh, before I forget," Flanders said. He took an envelope from inside his coat and handed it to me. On the outside in red pen was written, "Spenser, 1400." "The exchange rate is very good these days," Flanders said. "Your gain and our loss, isn't it."

I nodded and stuck the envelope in my jacket pocket. "Thank you," I said. "What have you got to tell me?"

"Let's order first," Flanders said. He had salmon, Downes had roast beef and I ordered mutton. Always try the native cuisine. The waiter looked like Barry Fitzgerald. He seemed delighted with our choices.

"Faith and begorra," I murmured.

Flanders said, "I beg your pardon?"

I shook my head. "Just an old American saying. What have you got?"

Downes said, "Really not much, I'm afraid. A group called Liberty has claimed responsibility for the Dixon murders and we have no reason to doubt them."

"What are they like?"

"Young people, apparently very conservative, recruited from all over western Europe. Headquarters might be in Amsterdam."

"How many?"

"Oh, ten, twelve. The figure changes every day. Some join, others leave. It doesn't seem a very well organized affair. More like a random group of juveniles larking about."

"Goals?"

"Excuse me?"

"What are the goals of their organization? Do they wish to save the great whales? Free Ireland? Smash apartheid? Restore Palestine? Discourage abortion?"

"I think they are anticommunist."

"That doesn't explain blowing Dixon up. Dixon industries aren't practicing state socialism, are they?"

Downes smiled and shook his head. "Hardly. The bombing was random violence. Urban guerrilla tactics. Disruption, terror, that sort of thing. It unravels the fabric of government, creates confusion, and allows the establishment of a new power structure. Or some such."

"How are they progressing?"

"The government seems to be holding its own."

"They do much of this sort of thing?"

"Hard to say," Downes sipped at his Scotch some more and rolled it around over his tongue. "Damned fine. It's hard to say because we get so bloody much of this sort of thing from so many corners. Gets difficult to know who is blowing up whom and why."

Flanders said, "But, as I understand it, Phil, this is not a major group. It doesn't threaten the stability of the country."

Downes shook his head, "No, surely not. Western civilization is in no immediate danger. But they do hurt people.

We all have reason to know that," Flanders said. "Does any of this help?"

"Not so far," I said. "If anything it hurts. As Downes knows, the more amateurish and unorganized and sappy a group like this is, the harder it is to get a handle on them. The big well organized ones I'll bet you people have infiltrated already."

Downes shrugged and sipped at his Scotch. "You're certainly right about the first part anyway, Spenser. The random childishness of it makes them much more difficult to deal with. The same random childishness limits their effectiveness in terms of revolution or whatever in hell they want. But it makes them damned hard to catch."

"Have you anything?"

"If you were from the papers," Downes said, "I'd reply that we were developing several promising possibilities. Since you're not from the papers I can be more brief. No. We haven't anything."

"No names? No faces?"

"Only the sketches we took from Mr. Dixon. We've circulated them. No one has surfaced."

"Informants?"

"No one knows anything about it."

"How hard have you been looking?"

"As hard as we can," Downes said. "You've not been over here long, but as you may know, we are pressed. The Irish business occupies most of our counterinsurgency machinery."

"You haven't looked hard."

Downes looked at Flanders. "Not true. We have given it as much attention as we can."

"I'm not accusing you of anything. I understand your kind of problems. I used to be a cop. I'm just saying it so Flanders will understand that you have not been able to conduct an exhaustive search. You've sifted the physical evidence. You've put out flyers, you've checked the urban guerrilla files and the case is still active. But you don't have a lot of bodies out beating the bushes on Egdon Heath or whatever.''

Downes shrugged and finished his Scotch. ''True,'' he said.

Barry Fitzgerald came back with food. He brought with him a man in a white apron who pushed a large copper-hooded steam table. At tableside he opened the hood, and carved to my specifications a large joint of mutton. When he was finished he stood back with a smile. I looked at Flanders. Flanders tipped him.

While the carver was carving, Barry put out the rest of the food. I ordered another beer. He seemed delighted to get it for me.

6

I rejected Flanders's offer of a cab and strolled back up the Strand toward the Mayfair in the slowly gathering evening. It was a little after eight o'clock. I had nowhere to be till morning and I walked randomly. Where the Strand runs into Trafalgar Square I turned down Whitehall. I stopped halfway down and looked at the two mounted sentries in the sentry box outside the Horse Guards building. They had leather hip boots and metal breastplates and old-time British Empire helmets, like statues, except for the young and ordinary faces that stared out under the helmets and the eyes that moved. The faces were kind of a shock. At the end of Whitehall was Parliament and Westminster Bridge, and across Parliament Square, Westminster Abbey. I'd walked through it some years back with Brenda Loring and a stampede of tourists. I'd like to walk through it when it was empty sometime.

I looked at my watch: 8:50. Subtract six hours, it was ten of three at home. I wondered if Susan was in her counseling class. It probably didn't meet every day. But maybe in the summer. I walked a little way out into Westminster Bridge and looked down at the river. The Thames. Jesus Christ. It had flowed through this city when only Wampanoags were on the Charles. Below me to the left was a landing platform where excursion boats loaded and unloaded. Susan and I had gone the year before to Amsterdam and had a wine and cheese cruise by candlelight along the canals and looked at the high seventeenth-century fronts of the canal houses. Shakespeare must have crossed this river. I had some vague recollection that the Globe Theatre was on the other side. Or had been. I also had the vague feeling that it no longer existed.

I looked at the river for a long time and then turned and leaned on the bridge railing with my arms folded and watched the people for a while. I was striking, I thought, in blue blazer, gray slacks, white oxford button-down and blue and red rep striped tie. I'd opened the tie and let it hang down casually against the white shirt, a touch of informality, and it was only a matter of time until a swinging London bird in a leather miniskirt saw that I was lonely and stopped to perk me up.

Miniskirts didn't seem prevalent. I saw a lot of harem pants and a lot of the cigarette look with Levis tucked into the top of high boots. I would have accepted either substitute, but no one made a move on me. Probably had found out I was foreign. Xenophobic bastards. No one even noticed the brass touch on the tassels on my loafers. Suze noticed them the first time I had them on.

I gave it up after a while. I hadn't smoked in ten or twelve years, but I wished then I'd had a cigarette that I could have taken a final drag on and flipped still burning into the river as I turned and walked away. Not smoking gains in the area of lung cancer, but it loses badly in the realm of dramatic gestures. At the edge of St. James's Park there was something called Birdcage Walk and I took it. Probably my Irish romanticism. It led me along the south side of St. James's Park to Buckingham Palace.

I stood outside awhile and stared in at the wide bare hard-paved courtyard. "How you doing, Queen," I murmured. There was a way to tell if they were there or not but I'd forgotten what it was. Didn't matter much. They probably wouldn't make a move on me either.

From the memorial statue in the circle in front of the palace a path led across Green Park toward Piccadilly and my hotel. I took it. I felt strange walking through a dark place of grass and trees an ocean away from home, alone. I thought about myself as a small boy and the circumstantial chain that connected that small boy with the middle-aging man who found himself alone in the night in a park in London. The little boy didn't seem to be me very much. And neither did the middle-aging man. I was incomplete. I missed Susan and I'd never missed anyone before.

I came out on Piccadilly again, turned right and then left onto Berkeley. I walked past the Mayfair and looked at Berkeley Square, long and narrow and very neat-looking. I didn't hear a nightingale singing. Someday maybe I'd come back here with Susan, and I would. I went back to the hotel and had room service bring me four beers.

"How many glasses, sir?"

"None," I said in a mean voice.

When it came I overtipped the bellhop to make up for the mean voice, drank the four beers from the bottle and went to bed.

In the morning I went out early and placed an ad in the *Times*. The ad said: "REWARD. One thousand pounds offered for information about organization called Liberty and death of three people in bombing of Steinlee's Restaurant last August 21. Call Spenser, Hotel Mayfair, London."

Downes had promised the previous evening to have the file on Dixon sent over to my hotel and by the time I got back it was there, in a brown manila envelope, folded in half the long way and crammed in the mail box back of the front desk. I took it up to my room and read it. There were

Xerox copies of the first officer's report, statements taken from witnesses, Dixon's statement from his hospital bed, copies of the Identikit sketches that had been made and regular reports of no progress submitted by various cops. There was also a Xerox of a note from Liberty claiming credit for the bombing and claiming victory over the "communist goons." And there was a copy of a brief history of Liberty, presumably culled from the newspaper files.

I lay on the bed in my hotel room with the airshaft window open and read it over three times, alert for clues the English cops had missed. There weren't any. If they had overlooked anything, I had too. It was almost as if I weren't any smarter than they were. I looked at my watch: 11:15. Almost time for lunch. If I went out and walked in leisurely fashion to a restaurant and ate slowly then I would have only four or five hours to kill till dinner. I looked at the material again. There was nothing in it. If my ad didn't produce any action, I didn't have any idea what to do next. I could drink a lot of beer and tour the country but Dixon might get restless about that after I'd gone through a couple of five grand advances.

I went out, went to a pub in Shepherd's Market near Curzon Street, had lunch, drank some beer, then walked up to Trafalgar Square and went into the National Gallery. I spent the afternoon there looking at the paintings, staring most of time at the portraits of people from another time and feeling the impact of their reality. The fifteenth-century woman in profile whose nose seemed to have been broken. Rembrandt's portrait of himself. I found myself straining after them. It was after five when I left and walked in a kind of head-buzzing sense of separateness out into Trafalgar Square and the current reality of the pigeons. The ad would run in the morning, they had told me. I had nothing to do tonight. I didn't feel like sitting alone in a restaurant and eating dinner, so I went back to my room, had a plateful of sandwiches sent up with some beer and ate in my room while I read my book.

The next morning the ad was there, as promised. As far as I could tell I was the only one who'd seen it. No one called that day, nor the next. The ad kept running. I hung around the hotel waiting until I got crazy, and then I went out and hoped they'd leave a message. During the next five days I visited the British Museum and looked at the Elgin Marbles, and visited the Tower of London and looked at the initials scratched in the walls of tower cells. I observed the changing of the guard, and jogged regularly through Hyde Park along the Serpentine.

I came in six days after the ad was placed, my shirt wet with sweat, my blue sweat pants worn stylishly with the ankle zippers open, my Adidas Cross-Countries still new-looking. I asked as always were there any messages, and the clerk said ''Yes'' and took a white envelope out of the box and gave it to me. It was sealed and said on it only ''Spenser.''

''This was delivered?'' I said.

''Yes, sir.''

''Not phoned in? This isn't your envelope?''

''No, sir, that was delivered by a young gentleman, I believe, sir. Perhaps half an hour ago.''

''Is he still here?'' I said.

''No, sir, I don't believe I see him about. You might try the coffee shop.''

''Thanks.''

Why hadn't they phoned it in? Because they wanted to see who I was, maybe, and they could do that by dropping off an envelope and posting someone to watch who opened it. Then they'd know who I was and I wouldn't know who they were. I walked toward one of the armchairs in the lobby where every afternoon tea was served. There was glass paneling on the far wall and I sat in a chair facing it so I could look in the mirror. I had on my sunglasses and I peeked out from behind them at the mirror while I opened the envelope. It was thin and unsuspicious. I doubted a letter bomb. For all I knew it might be a note from Flanders inviting me to join him for high tea at the Connaught. But it wasn't. It was what I wanted.

The note said, "Be at the cafeteria end of the east tunnel near the north gate entrance to the London Zoo in Regent's Park tomorrow at ten in the morning."

I pretended to read it again and surveyed the lobby from behind my shades as far as the mirror would let me. I didn't see anything suspicious, but I didn't expect to. I was trying to memorize all the faces in the place so if I saw one again I'd remember it. I put the letter back in the envelope and turned thoughtfully in my chair, tapping my teeth with a corner of the envelope. Pensive, deep in thought, looking hard as a bastard around the hotel lobby. No one was carrying a Sten gun. I went out the front door and strolled up toward Green Park.

It is not easy to follow someone without being spotted, if the someone is trying to catch you doing it. I caught her crossing Piccadilly. She'd been in the hotel lobby buying postcards, and now she was crossing Piccadilly toward Green Park half a block down the street. I was still in my sweat pants and I didn't have a gun. They might want to burn me right now right quick once they had me spotted.

In Green Park I stopped, did a few deep knee bends and stretching exercises for show and then started an easy jog down toward the Mall. If she wanted me she'd have to run to keep up. If she started running to keep up, I'd know she didn't care about being spotted, which would mean she was probably going to shoot me, or point me out to someone else who would shoot me. In which case I would bang a U-turn and run like hell for Piccadilly and a cop.

She didn't run. She let me go, and by the time I reached the Mall she was gone. I walked back up to Piccadilly along Queen's Walk, crossed the street and walked down to the Mayfair. I didn't see her and she wasn't in the lobby. I went up to my room and took a shower with my gun lying on the top of the toilet tank. I felt good. After a week of watching the sun set on the British Empire I was working again. And I was one up on somebody who thought they were one up on me. If she was from Liberty then they thought they had me spotted and I didn't know them. If they weren't, if they wanted just to see if they could screw me out of the thousand pounds and were taking a look at how hard I looked, I was still even. I knew them and they thought I didn't, and moreover they thought that's where they were. There were drawbacks. They knew all of me and I only knew one of them. On the other hand, I was a professional and they were amateurs. Of course, if one of them laid a bomb on me, the bomb might not know the difference between amateurs and professionals.

I put on jeans, a white Levi shirt, and white Adidas Roms with blue stripes. I didn't want the goddamned limeys to think an American sleuth didn't know color coordination. I got a black woven-leather shoulder rig out of the suitcase and slipped into it. They aren't as comfortable as hip holsters, but I wanted to wear a short Levi jacket and the hip holster would show. I put my gun in the holster and put on the Levi jacket, and left it unbuttoned. It was dark blue corduroy. I looked at myself in the mirror over the bureau. I turned up the collar. Elegant. Clean-shaven, fresh-showered, with a recent haircut. I was the image of the international adventurer. I tried a couple of fast draws to make sure the shoulder holster worked right, did one perfect Bogart imitation at myself in the mirror, "All right, Louis, drop the gun," and I was ready for action.

The room had been made up already so there was no need for a maid to come in again. I took a can of talcum powder and, standing in the hall, I sprinkled it carefully and evenly over the rug in front of the door inside my room. Anyone who came in would leave a footprint inside and tracks outside when he left. If they were observant they might notice and wipe out the tracks. But unless they were carrying a can of talc they would have trouble covering the footprints inside.

I shut the door carefully over the smooth layer of talcum and took the can with me. There was a wastebasket by the elevators and I dropped the empty talc can in. I'd get another on my way back tonight.

I walked down to Piccadilly Circus and took a subway to Regent's Park. I had my map of London folded and creased in my hip pocket and I got it out and sneaked a look at it, trying not to look just like a tourist. I figured out the best walk through the park, nodded knowingly in case anyone was watching, as if I was just confirming what I knew already, and headed on up to the north gate. I wanted a look at the territory before I showed up there tomorrow.

I went past the cranes, geese, and owls at north gate entrance and across the bridge over Regent's Canal. A water bus chugged by underneath. By the insect house a tunnel led under a zoo office building and emerged beside the zoo restaurant. To the left was a cafeteria. To the right a restaurant and bar. Past the cafeteria were some flamingos in a little grass park. Flamingos on the grass, alas. If they wanted to burn me, the tunnel was their best bet. It wasn't much of a tunnel, but it was straight and without alcoves. No place to hide. If someone came at me from each end they could put me in two without much trouble. Stay out of the tunnel.

At the photo shop in the cafeteria I bought a guide to the zoo that had a map inside the back cover. The south gate, down by Wolf Wood, looked like a good spot to come in tomorrow. I walked down to take a look. Past the parrot house and across from something labeled *Budgerigars*, there were kids taking camel rides and shrieking with laughter at the camel's rolling asymmetrical gait.

The south gate was just past the birds of prey aviary, which seemed ominous, past the wild dogs and foxes, and next to the Wolf Wood. That wasn't too encouraging either. I went back up and looked at the cafeteria setup. There was a pavilion and tables. The food was served from an open-faced arcadelike building. If I sat on the pavilion at an open-air table I was a good target from almost any point. There was little cover. I ordered a steak and kidney pudding from the cafeteria and took it to a table. It was cold and tasted like a Nerf ball. While I gagged it down, I looked at my situation. If they were going to shoot me, there was little to prevent them. Maybe they weren't going to shoot me, but I couldn't plan much on that.

"You can't plan on the enemy's intentions," I said. "You have to plan on what he can do, not what he might."

A boy cleaning the tables looked at me oddly. "Beg pardon, sir?"

"Just remarking on military strategy. Ever do that? Sit around and talk to yourself about military strategy?"

"No, sir."

"You're probably wise not to. Here, take this with you."

I dropped most of my steak and kidney pie into his trash bucket. He moved on. I wanted two things, maybe three, depending on how you counted. I wanted not to get killed. I wanted to decommission some of the enemy. I wanted at least one of them to get away with me following. Decommission. Nice word. Sounds better than kill. But I am thinking about killing a couple of people here. Calling it decommission isn't going to make it better. It's their choice though. I won't shoot if I'm not taking fire. They try to kill me, I'll fight. I'm not setting them up. They are setting me up . . . Except I'm setting them up to set me up so I can set them up. Messy. But you're going to do it anyway, kid, whether it's messy or not, so there's not too much point to analyzing its ethical implications. Yeah, I guess I am. I guess I'll just see if it feels good afterward.

They were experienced with explosives. And they didn't worry about who got hurt. We knew that. If I were they I might wait till I got inside the tunnel, then roll in some explosives and turn me into a cave painting. Or they could do me in on the bridge over the canal.

I knew who they were. I knew the girl and I had the pictures that Dixon had given me. Only the girl knew who I was. She'd have to be there to spot me. Maybe I could spot them first. How many would they send? If they were going to trap me in the tunnel, at least two plus the spotter. They'd at least want one at each end. But when they blew up the Dixons there were nine of them that Dixon spotted. They didn't need nine. It must have been their sense of community. The group that blasts together lasts together.

My bet was they'd show up in force. And they'd be careful. They'd be looking for a police setup. Anyone would. They wouldn't be that stupid. So they'd be watching too. I stood up. There was nothing to do but blunder into it. I'd stay out of the tunnel, and I'd keep away from open areas as best I could, and I'd look very carefully at everything. I knew them and they didn't know it. Only one of them knew me. That was as much edge as I was going to get. The shoulder holster under my coat felt awkward. I wished I had more fire power.

The steak and kidney pie felt like a bowling ball in my stomach as I headed out onto Prince Albert Road and caught a red double-decker bus back to Mayfair.

7

On the way back to my hotel I got off the bus on Piccadilly and went into a men's specialty store. I bought a
blond wig, a blond mustache, and some make-up cement
to attach it. Spenser, man of a thousand faces. Outside my
door there was a white talcum powder footprint. I kept on
going past my room and on down the corridor. When it
intersected with a cross corridor I turned right and leaned
against the wall. There was no sign of anyone lurking. A
standard approach to this kind of business would be one on
the inside and one on the outside, but that didn't seem the
case.

Of course it could have been a hotel employee on
innocent business. But it might be someone who wanted to
shoot me dead. I put the bag with my disguise in it on the
floor and slid my gun out of the shoulder holster. I held it
in my right hand and folded my arms across my chest so
the gun was concealed under my arm. There was no one in
the corridor. I peeked around the corner. There was no one
in that corridor either.

I went down the corridor softly to my room. Took the
key out of my pocket with my left hand; my right had the
gun in it, chest-high now, and visible. The dim sounds of
the hotel's muffled machinery whirred on around me. The
elevators going and stopping. The sound of air-conditioning

apparatus, faintly a television playing somewhere. The hotel door was dark oak, the room numbers in brass.

I stood outside my room and listened. There was no sound. Standing to the right of the door and reaching with my left hand, I put the key as gently as I could into the lock and turned it. Nothing happened. I opened the door a fraction to free the catch. Then I wiggled the key out, and slipped it back in my pocket. I took a deep breath. It was hard to swallow. I shoved the door open with my left hand and rolled back out of sight against the wall to the right of the door. I had the hammer back on my gun. Nothing happened. No one made a sound.

The lights were off, but the afternoon sun was shining and the room shed some light into the corridor. I edged a few steps down the corridor so that I could get a better angle on the door, and crossed. If someone came out shooting they'd expect me to be where I had been, to the right of the door, on the same wall. I folded my arms again to hide the gun, and leaned against the wall and looked at the open door and waited.

The elevator stopped to my right and a man in a tattersall vest got off with a lady in a pink pantsuit. He was bald, her hair was bluish gray. They looked past me, rigorously not being curious as they walked by. They were equally careful not to look into the open door of the room. I watched them as they went on. They didn't look like bombers but who can tell a bomber by his appearance. You have to be a little suspicious of anyone who wears a tattersall vest anyway. They went into a room about ten doors down. Nothing else moved.

I would feel like a terrible numb-nuts if the room turned out to be empty and I was poised out here like agent X-15 for hours. But I would be a terrible numb-nuts if I just walked in there and found it flourishing with assassins, and bought the farm right here in Merry England because I wasn't patient. I would wait.

He would wait, too, apparently. But I was betting the tension would get him. The open door would get wider and wider open as he looked at it. If there were two of them it would take longer. One guy gets scareder than two guys. But I had nowhere to go till ten next morning. I was betting I could wait longer.

An Indian woman in a white uniform rolled a laundry cart past me, looked curiously into the open room but paid me no attention. I was finding that more and more women were paying me no attention these days. Perhaps tastes were drifting away from the matinee idol type.

The light from my room waned. I kept my eyes on it because I knew there'd be a shadow when the assassin made his move. Or maybe he knew that too and was waiting till dark.

Two African men came off the elevator and walked down past me. They both wore gray business suits with very narrow lapels. They both wore dark narrow ties and white broadcloth shirts with collars that turned up slightly at the ends. The one nearest me had tribal marks scarred into his cheeks. His companion had round gold-framed glasses on. They were speaking in British-accented English as they went by me, and paid no attention to me or the door. I watched them peripherally as I watched the door too. Anyone could be an accomplice.

The phone was near the door, and in the reeking silence I was pretty sure that the assassin couldn't call without me hearing him. But there might have been a signal of some sort from the window, or there might be a prearranged time when if he didn't call the back-up came looking.

It was hard watching both the door and the corridor traffic. I was getting tired of holding the gun. My hand was stiff, and with the thing cocked I had to hold it carefully. I thought about shifting it to my left hand. I wasn't as good with my left hand, and I might need to be very good all of a sudden. I wouldn't be too good if my gun hand had gone to sleep, however. I shifted the thing to my left hand and exercised my right. The gun felt clumsy in my left. I ought to practice left-handed more. I hadn't anticipated a gun hand going to sleep. *How'd you get shot, Spenser? Well, it's this way, Saint Pete. I was staked out in a hotel corridor but my hand went to sleep. Then after a while my entire body nodded off. Did Bogie's hand ever go to sleep, Spenser? Did Kerry Drake's? No, sir, I don't think we can admit you here to Private-Eye Heaven, Spenser.*

I was getting soft standing out there in the corridor. My right hand felt better and I shifted the gun back. No more light came out of the open door of my room. A family of four, complete with Instamatics and shoulder bags, came out of the elevator and walked past me down the corridor. The kids looked into the open door. The father said, "Keep walking." He had an American accent and his voice was tired. The mom had an admirable backside. They turned right at the cross corridor and disappeared. It was getting late. I was working overtime here. Sudden-death overtime. Ah, Spenser, what a way you have with words. Sudden-death overtime. Dynamite.

My feet hurt. I was beginning to experience lower back pain from standing so long. Why do you get more tired standing than walking? An imponderable. Waiting for someone to jump out of a dark doorway and shoot at you is tiring too. Pay attention. Don't let the mind wander. You tended to lose sight for a minute when the mom with the backside walked past. If that had been fight time you'd have cashed it in right there, kid.

I looked hard at the door. The assassin would have to

appear from the right. The open door was flush against the left-hand wall. He'd roll around the right wall looking for me down the corridor. Or maybe not, maybe he'd come on his belly, close to the floor. That's what I would do. Or would I? Maybe I'd dive out of the door and get an angle on me from across the corridor, try to be too quick for the guy who's been standing there getting hypnotized by staring at the door.

Or maybe I wouldn't even be there. Maybe I would be an empty room and some nervous dimwit would stand outside and stare at the emptiness for a number of hours. I could call hotel security and tell them I'd found my door open. But if there was someone in there the first person through the door was going to get blasted. The assassin had been in there too long to make fine distinctions. And if he was a Liberty type he didn't care much who got killed anyway. I couldn't ask someone else to walk in there for me. I'd wait. I could wait. It was one of the things I was good at. I could hang on.

Up the corridor past me a room service waiter, dark-skinned in a white coat, wheeled a table full of covered dishes off the service elevator and around the corner to the right. A faint baked potato smell drifted back down the corridor to me. After my steak and kidney pie I had thought about extensive fasting, but the baked potato smell made me reconsider.

The assassin came out in a scrabbling crouch, and fired one shot down the corridor toward the elevator on the wall opposite to where I was, before he realized I wasn't there. He was quick, and half turned to shoot toward me when I shot him in the chest, my arm straight, my body half turned, not breathing while I squeezed off the shot. At close range my bullet spun him half around. I shot him again as he fell on his side with his knees up. The gun skittered out of his hand as he fell. Small caliber. Long barrel. Target gun. I jumped over and dove through the open door of my room, landed on my shoulder and rolled past the bed. There was a second man, and his first bullet took a piece out of the door frame behind me. His second one caught me with a sharp tug in the back of my left thigh. Half sitting, I shot three times into the middle of his dark form, in faint silhouette against the window. He went backward over a straight chair and lay on his back with one foot draped on the chair seat.

I raised to a full sit-up against the wall. That's why they could wait so long. There were two. My breath was coming very heavy and I could feel my heart pumping in the middle of my chest. I'm not gonna get shot, I'm gonna have cardiac arrest some day.

I took in deep breaths of air. In the right-hand breast pocket of my blue corduroy Levi jacket were twelve extra shells. I opened the cylinder of my gun and popped out the spent cartridges. There was one live round left. I felt down at the back of my left leg. It didn't hurt yet, but it was warm and I knew I was bleeding. The gun shots in the enclosed corridor had been very loud. That should bring some cops pretty quick.

I edged over to the dark shape with his foot on the chair. I felt for pulse and found none. I got to my feet and walked a little unsteadily to the door. The first man I shot lay as he had fallen. The long-barreled target pistol a foot from his inert hand. His knees drawn up. There was blood on the hall carpet. I put my gun back in its holster and walked over to him. He was dead too. I went back into my room. The back of my leg was beginning to hurt. I sat down on the bed and picked up the phone when I heard the footsteps in the hall. Some of them stopped a little way from my room and some came on to the door. I put the phone back down.

"All right in there, come out with your hands up. This is the police."

"It's okay," I said. "There's a guy dead in here and I'm wounded. Come on in. I'm on your side."

A young man in a light raincoat stepped quickly into the room and pointed a revolver at me. Behind him came an older man with graying hair and he pointed a revolver at me too.

"Stand up, please," the younger man said, "and put your hands on top of your head, fingers clasped."

"There's a gun in the shoulder holster under my left arm," I said. Several uniformed bobbies and two more guys in civilian clothes crowded into the room. One of them went directly to the phone and began to talk. The guy with the graying hair patted me down, took my gun, took the seven remaining bullets from my jacket pocket and stepped back.

The young one said to the man on the phone, "He's bleeding. He'll need medical attention." The guy on the phone nodded.

The young cop said to me, "All right, tell us about it, please."

"I'm a good guy," I said. "I'm an American investigator. I'm over here working on a case. If you'll get hold of Inspector Downes in your department he'll vouch for me."

"And these gentlemen," he nodded at the body on the floor and included, with a sweep of his chin, the guy I had dumped in the corridor.

"I don't know. I'd guess they were going to put me away because I was on this case. I came back to the room and they were waiting for me."

The gray cop said, "You killed them both?"

"Yeah."

"This is the gun?"

"Yeah."

"Some identification, please?"

I handed it over, including the British gun permit.

The gray cop said to the one on the phone, "Tell them to get hold of Phil Downes. We've got an American investigator here named Spenser that claims to know him."

The cop on the phone nodded. As he talked he stuck a cigarette in his mouth and lit it.

A man came in with a small black doctor bag. He had on a dark silk suit and a lavender shirt with the collar spread out over the suit lapels. Around his neck were small turquoise beads on a choker necklace.

"Name's Kensy," he said. "Hotel physician."

"You staid British doctors are all the same," I said.

"No doubt. Please drop your pants and lie across the bed, face down."

I did what I was told. The leg was hurting a lot now, and I knew the back of my pants leg was soaked with blood. Dignity is not easy, I thought. But it is always possible. The doctor went into the bathroom to wash.

The cop in the light raincoat said, "You know either of these people, Mr. Spenser?"

"I haven't even gotten a look at them yet."

The doctor came back. I couldn't see him but I could hear him fumbling around. "This may sting a bit." I smelled alcohol and felt it sting as the doctor swabbed off the area.

"The bullet still in there?" I asked.

"No, went right through. Clean wound. Some blood loss, but nothing, I think, to be concerned over."

"Good, I'd just as soon not be carrying a slug around in the upper thigh," I said.

"You may choose to call it that if you wish," the doctor said, "but in point of face, my man, you've been shot in the arse."

"There's marksmanship," I said. "And in the dark too."

8

The doctor put a pressure bandage on my, ah, thigh, and gave me some pills for the pain. "You'll walk funny for a few days," he said. "After that you should be fine. Though you'll have an extra dimple in your cheeks now."

"I'm glad there's socialized medicine," I said. "If only there was a vow of silence that went with it."

Downes showed up as the doctor was leaving. And he and I explained my situation to the gray cop and the young one. Two guys came with body bags and before they took away the bodies we looked at them. I got out my Identikit pictures and both of them were in the pictures. Neither one was out of his twenties. Or ever would be.

Downes looked at the Identikit picture and the fallen kid, and nodded. "How much you get for him?"

"Twenty-five hundred dollars."

"What will that buy in your country?"

"Half a car."

"Luxury car?"

"No."

Downes looked at the kid again. He had long blond hair and his fingernails were very recently clipped and clean. His still hands looked very vulnerable.

"Half an inexpensive car," Downes said.

"He ambushed me," I said. "I didn't lay in wait for either of them."

"You say."

"Oh come on, Downes. Is this the way I'd do it?"

Downes shrugged. He was looking at the traces of talcum powder still in front of the door. White partial footprints were now all over the room.

"You powdered the room before you left," he said.

"Yeah."

"If one of them hadn't?"

"I'd have opened the door very slowly and carefully and checked the floor inside before I went in," I said.

"And you waited them out. Shoved the door open and stood in the corridor until they made their move."

"Yeah."

"Well now, you're intrepid enough, aren't you."

"The very word for it," I said.

"The problem is," Downes said, "we can't have you running around London shooting down suspected anarchists at random and collecting the bounty."

"That's not my plan, Downes. I don't shoot people I don't have to shoot. I'm here doing a job that needs to be done, that you people are too busy to do. These two clowns tried to kill me, remember. I didn't shoot them because they were suspected anarchists. I shot them to keep them from shooting me."

"Why did you powder the floor when you left?"

"Can't be too careful in a foreign land," I said.

"And the ad you placed in the *Times*?"

I shrugged. "I had to get their attention."

"Apparently you succeeded."

A uniformed cop came in with my bag of disguises and handed it to Downes. "Found this down the corridor, sir, around the corner."

"That's mine," I said. "I left it there when I discovered the assassins."

"Assassins, is it," Downes said. He reached in the bag and took out my wig and mustache and make-up cement. His broad placid face brightened. He smiled a large smile that pushed his cheeks up and made his eyes almost close. He held the mustache under his nose. "How do I look, Grimes?" he said to the bobby.

"Like a ruddy guardsman, sir."

"My ass is hurting," I said. "And I don't think it's the wound."

"Why a disguise, Spenser? Did they know who you were?"

"I think one of them spotted me yesterday."

"And you arranged a meeting?"

I didn't want Downes at the meeting. I was afraid he'd scare off my quarry and I needed to make another contact.

"No, they just left a letter in my mailbox and when they saw me take it and read it they knew who I was. There's no meeting yet. The letter said they'd be in touch. I think it was a setup. So I thought I'd change my appearance a bit."

Downes looked at me silently for maybe a minute.

"Well," he said, "certainly there will be little grieving over these two. I do hope you'll keep in touch with us as things develop. And I do hope that you do not plan to bring all of these people to justice this way."

"Not if I have a choice," I said.

The technicians zipped up the second body bag and trundled it out on a dolly.

"Half an inexpensive car," Downes said.

"What kind of gun did the guy in here have? The one that shot me?"

The cop in the light raincoat said, "Same as the one in

the hall, Colt twenty-two target pistol. They probably stole a crate of them somewhere. You're lucky they didn't steal a forty-five caliber, or a Magnum.''

"Might have taken a good deal more of your butt than it did," Downes said.

"Thigh," I said. "Upper thigh wound."

Downes shrugged. "I'd lock my door if I were you, and be quite alert, all right?''

I nodded. Downes and the other two were all that were left in the room now.

"Keep in touch, won't you?'' Downes said.

I nodded again. Downes gestured at the door with his head and the three of them got up and left. I closed the door behind them and slid the bolt. The doctor had given me some pills for the pain if it got bad. I didn't want to take them yet. I needed to think. I sat on the bed and changed my mind quickly. Lying was a better idea. Lying on my stomach was the best idea of all. Shot in the ass. Susan would doubtless find that funny. Only hurts when I laugh.

This was not a dumb group. They had me thinking about tomorrow and while I was thinking about tomorrow they would ace me tonight. Not bad. But now what. Would they show up tomorrow? Yes. They would be there looking to see if I were there looking to see if they were there. I couldn't know that tonight's trouble was them. They didn't know I had Identikit drawings. Even if I did, I wouldn't know—hell, I didn't know—that the people who wanted to see me were the same ones who tried to blow me away tonight. Maybe there really was an informant. Maybe tonight's people were trying to stop me from getting to the informant. I'd have to go tomorrow.

I left a wake-up call for seven-thirty, took two painkillers, and in a little while I went to sleep on my stomach. It was a pill and pain sleep, fitful, and full of brief awakenings. Killing two kids didn't help any. I was up before the wake-up call, relieved at the dawn, feeling like I'd backed into a stove. I had slept in my clothes and my pants were stiff with dried blood when I took them off. I showered and did my best to keep the bandage dry. I brushed my teeth and shaved and put on clean clothes. Gray slacks, blue-and-white-striped shirt with a button-down collar, blue knit tie, black-tasseled loafers, shoulder holster with gun. Continuity in the midst of change. I pasted on my fake mustache, adjusted my wig, put on a pair of pink-tinted aviator glasses and slid into my blue blazer with the brass buttons and the full tattersall lining. You *can* trust a guy with a tattersall lining. I checked the mirror. The roll in my collar wasn't quite right. I loosened the tie and redid it not quite as tight.

I stepped back for a look in the full-length mirror. I looked like the bouncer in a gay bar. But it might do. I looked a lot different than I had yesterday in sweat pants and track shoes in the lobby. I put six more bullets in my inside coat pocket and I was ready. I powdered the floor again, and went to the hotel coffee shop. I hadn't eaten since the steak and kidney pudding and it was past time. I ate three eggs sunny side up and ham and coffee and toast. It was eight-ten when I got through. In front of the hotel I got a cab and rode up to the zoo in comfort. Leaning a little to the right as I sat.

9

They were there. The girl I'd spotted before was looking at the flamingos as I walked up from the south gate past the hawks and eagles in the birds of prey displays. I stopped with my back to her and looked at the parrots in the parrot house. She didn't know I had spotted her before so she made no attempt to hide. She just looked casual as she strolled over to the crows' cage. She didn't take any note of me. Spenser, master illusionist.

For the next two hours we did something difficult and complex like the ritual mating dance of ring-necked pheasants. She looked for me without appearing to and I watched her without appearing to. There had to be some others around. People with guns. They didn't know what I looked like, though they probably had a description. I didn't really know what they looked like unless the Identikit drawings were very accurate and they were the same people who had wasted the Dixons.

She strolled to the chimps' lawn. I strolled to the cockatoos. She walked to the parrots, I moved to the north end of the gibbons' cage. She looked at the budgies while keeping an eye out for me. I had a cup of coffee at the garden kiosk while making sure I didn't lose her. She was wondering if there were undercover cops around. I was looking for members of her group. We were both trying to look like ordinary zoo patrons who chose to stay around the east tunnel area of the zoo. My part was complicated by the fact that I felt like a horse's ass with my wig and my mustache. I was having a little trouble with the coffee because of the mustache. If it fell off that might give the bad guys a hint that something was up.

The strain of it was physical. By eleven o'clock I was sweating and the back of my neck hurt. My wound was hurting all the time. And not limping was a matter of concentration all the time. It must have been hard for her too, though she hadn't been shot in the back of the lap. As far as I knew.

She was a pretty good-looking person. Not as young as the people I'd met last night. Thirty maybe, with straight hair, very blond that reached her shoulders. Her eyes were very round and noticeable, and as close as I'd gotten they looked black. Her breasts were a little too large but her thighs were first quality. She had on black sandals and white slacks and a white open-necked blouse with a black scarf knotted at the neck. She had a big black leather shoulder bag, and I was betting a gun in it. Handgun probably. The bag wasn't quite big enough for an antitank gun.

At eleven-forty-five by the clock tower she gave up. I was nearly two hours late. She shook her head twice, vigorously, at someone I couldn't see and headed for the tunnel. I went after her. The tunnel was something I wanted to avoid, but I didn't see how I could. I didn't want to lose her. I'd gone to a lot of trouble for this contact and I wanted to get something out of it. But if they caught me in the tunnel I was dead. I had no choice. Disguise, do your duty. I went into the tunnel after her.

There was no one in it. I walked through slowly, whistling and unconcerned, with the trapezius muscles across my back in a state of tension. As I came out of the tunnel I ditched the pink-shaded glasses in a trash basket and put on my normal sunglasses. I took my tie off and stuck it in my pocket and opened the collar of my shirt three buttons. I read in a Dick Tracy Crime Stopper that a small change in appearance can be helpful when following someone surreptitiously.

She wasn't hard to follow. She wasn't looking for me. And she was walking. She walked east on Prince Albert Road and turned down Albany Street. We went south on Albany across Marylebone onto Great Portland Street.

To the left the Post Office Tower stuck up above the city. She turned left ahead of me and started up Carburton Street. The area was getting more neighborhood and small grocery store. More middle class and student. I had a dim memory that east of the Post Office Tower was Bloomsbury and the University of London and the British Museum. She turned right onto Cleveland Street. She had a hell of a walk. I liked to watch it and I had been now for ten or fifteen minutes. It was a free, long-striding, hip-swing walk with a lot of spring to it. It was fast pace for walking wounded, and I felt the gunshot wound with every step. At the corner of Tottenham Street, diagonally across from a hospital, she turned into one of the brick-faced buildings, up three steps and in the front door.

I found a doorway with some sun and stood in it, and leaned against the wall where I could see the door she'd gone in, and waited. She didn't come out until almost two-thirty in the afternoon. Then it was just to walk half a block to a grocery store and back with a bag of groceries. I never had to leave my doorway.

Okay, I thought, this is where she lives. So what? One of the things about my employment was the frequency with which I didn't know what I was doing or what to do next. Always a fresh surprise. I have tracked the beast to its lair, I thought. Now what do I do with her? Beast wasn't the right word, but it didn't sound right to say I've tracked the beauty to her lair.

As so often in dilemmas of this kind, I came upon the perfect thing to do. Nothing. I decided I'd better wait and watch and see what happened. If at first you don't succeed put it off till tomorrow. I looked at my watch. After four. I had been watching the girl and her doorway since before nine this morning. Every natural appetite and need pressed upon me. I was hungry and thirsty and nearly incontinent and the pain in my backside was both real and symbolic. If I was going to do this for very long I was going to need help. By six I had to pitch it in.

It was less than two blocks from the Post Office Tower. They had most of what I needed and I headed for it. On the way I took off my wig and mustache and stuffed them in my pocket. The dining room opened at six twenty and the second thing I did after I reached it was to get a table by the window and order a beer. The restaurant was on top of the tower and rotated slowly so that in the course of a meal you saw the whole 360-degree panorama of London from much the highest building. I knew that rotating restaurants like this atop a garish skyscraper were supposed to be touristy and cheap and I tried to be scornful of it. But the view of London below me was spectacular, and I finally gave up and loved it. Furthermore, the restaurant carried Amstel, which I could no longer get at home, and to celebrate I had several bottles. It was midweek and early and the restaurant wasn't yet crowded. No one hurried me.

The menu was large and elaborate and seemed devoid of steak and kidney pudding. That in itself was worth another drink. As the restaurant inched around I could look south at the Thames and to the east at St. Paul's with its massive dome, squat and Churchillian, so different from the upward soar of the great continental cathedrals. Its feet were planted firmly in the English bedrock. I was beginning to feel the four Dutch beers on an empty stomach. Here's looking at you, St. Paul's, I said to myself.

The waiter took my order and brought me another beer. I sipped it. Regent's Park edged into view from the north. There was a lot of green in this huge city. This sceptered isle, this England. I drank some more beer. Here's looking at you, Billy boy. The waiter brought my veal piccata and I ate it without biting his hand, but just barely. For dessert I had an English trifle and two cups of coffee, and it was after eight before I was out on the street heading for home.

There had been enough beer to make my wound feel okay and I wanted to walk off the indulgence, so I brought out my London street map and plotted a pleasant stroll back to Mayfair. It took me down Cleveland to Oxford Street, west on Oxford and then south on New Bond Street. It was after nine and the beer had worn off when I turned up Bruton Street to Berkeley Square. The walk had settled the food and drink, but my wound was hurting again and I was thinking about a hot shower and clean sheets. Ahead of me up Berkeley Street was the side door of the Mayfair. I went in past the hotel theater, up two stairs into the lobby. I saw no one in the lobby with a lethal engine. The elevator was crowded and unthreatening. I went up two floors above mine and got off and walked down toward the far end of the corner and took the service elevator, marked EMPLOYEES ONLY, to my floor.

No sense walking like a fly into the parlor. The service elevator opened into a little foyer where linen was stored. Four doors down toward my room from the service elevator the cross corridor intersected. Leaning near the corner and occasionally peering out around the corner down toward my door was a fat man with kinky blond hair and rosy cheeks. He was wearing a gray gabardine raincoat and he kept his right hand in the pocket. He didn't have to be waiting to ambush me but I couldn't think what else he'd be doing there. Where was the other one? They'd send two, or more, but not one.

He should be at the other end of my corridor so they could get me in a crossfire. They would know who I was when I stopped and put the key in my door. I stood very quietly inside the linen foyer and watched. At the far end of the corridor the elevator doors slid back and three people got out, two young women and a fortyish man in a three-piece corduroy suit. As they came down the corridor toward me a man appeared beyond the elevator and watched them. All three passed my door and the guy down the corridor disappeared. The one closer to me turned and looked down the cross corridor as if he were waiting for his wife.

Okay, so they were trying again. Industrious bastards. Hostile, too. All I did was put an ad in the paper. I got back in the service elevator and went up three floors. I got out, went down an identical corridor to the public elevators and looked in behind them. The stairway was there. I descended around the elevator shaft and it was in the stairway that the other shooter was hiding three floors below. I'd take him from above. He wouldn't be looking for me to come down. He'd be waiting for me to come up.

I took off my coat, rolled my sleeves back over the elbows and took off my shoes and socks. It was psychological on the sleeves, I admit, but they bothered me and made me feel encumbered, and so what if I humor a fetish. The fifty-dollar black-tasseled loafers were lovely to look at, delightful to own, but awful to fight in, and they made noise when you snuck up on assassins. Stocking feet tend to be slippery. With my shoes off, my cuffs dragged and I had to roll them up. I looked like I was going wading. Huck Finn.

I went down the stairs in my bare feet without a sound. The stairshaft was neat and empty. To my right the workings of the elevator purred and halted, purred and halted. At the bend before my floor I stopped and listened. I heard someone sniff, and the sound of fabric scraping against the wall. He was on my side of the fire door. He listened for the elevator stop, and if it was this floor he'd step out after the doors closed and take a look. That made it easier. He was leaning against the wall. That was the fabric scrape I heard. He'd be facing the fire doors, leaning against the wall. He'd want the gun hand free. Unless he was left-handed that meant he'd be on the left-hand wall. Most people weren't left-handed.

I stepped around the corner and there he was, four steps down, leaning against the left-hand wall with his back to me. I jumped the four steps and landed behind him just as he caught a reflected movement in the wired-glass fire doors. He half turned, pulling the long-barreled gun out of his waistband, and I hit him with my forearm across the right side of the face, high. He bounced back against the wall, and fell over on the floor, and was quiet. You break your hand hitting a man in the head hard enough to put him out. I picked up the gun. Part of the same shipment. Long barreled .22 target gun. Not a lot of pizzazz, but if they shot the right part of you they would do. I felt him over for another weapon, but the .22 was it.

I ran back up the two flights, put my shoes and jacket back on, rolled down my pants legs, stuffed the pistol in my belt at the small of my back and ran back downstairs. My man was not moving. He lay on his back with his mouth open. I noticed he had those whiskers like one of the Smith Brothers that starts at the corner of the mouth and runs back to the ears. Ugly.

I opened the fire door and stepped into the hall. The man in the other corridor wasn't visible. I walked straight down the hall past my door. I could sense a slight movement at the corner of the corridor. I turned the corridor corner and he was standing a little uncertainly, trying to look unconcerned but half suspicious. I must look like his description, but why hadn't I gone into my room. His hand was still in his raincoat pocket. The raincoat was open.

I walked past him three steps, turned around and yanked the open raincoat down over his arms. He struggled to get his arm out of his pocket. Without letting go of his coat I took the gun out from under my arm with my right hand and pressed it into the hollow behind his ear. "England swings," I said, "like a pendulum do."

10

"Take your right hand about one inch out of your pocket," I said, "and stop."

He did. There was no gun in it. "Okay, now put both hands behind your back and clasp them." I let go of his coat with my left hand and reached around and took the pistol out of his pocket. Target gun number four. I stuck it in my left-hand jacket pocket where it sagged very unfashionably. I patted him down quickly with my left hand. He didn't have another piece.

"Very good. Now put both hands back in your pockets."

He did.

"What's your name?"

"Suck my ass," he said.

"Okay, Suck," I said. "We're going down the corridor and pick up your buddy. If you have an itch, don't scratch it. If you hiccup or sneeze or yawn or bat your eyes I am going to shoot a hole through your head." I held the back of his collar with my left hand and kept the muzzle of my gun pressed in behind his right ear and we walked down the corridor. Past the elevator, behind the fire doors there was nobody. I hadn't hit him hard enough and whiskers was up and away. He didn't have a weapon and I didn't think he'd try me without one. I had already killed two of his buddies armed.

"Suck, my boy," I said, "I think you've been forsaken. But I won't turn my back on you. We'll go to my place and rap."

"Don't call me Suck, you bloody bastard." His English sounded upper class but not quite native.

I took out my room key and gave it to him. The gun still at his neck. "Open the door, Scum Bag, and step in."

He did. No bomb went off. I went in after him and kicked the door shut.

"Sit there," I said and shoved him toward the armchair near the airshaft.

He sat. I put the gun back in my shoulder holster. Put the two target pistols on the top shelf of the closet, took my wig and mustache and tie out of my pockets, took off my blue blazer and hung it up.

"What's your name?" I said.

He stared at me without speaking.

"You English?"

He was silent.

"Do you know that I get twenty-five hundred dollars for you alive or dead, and dead is easier?"

He crossed one pudgy leg over the other one and locked his hands over his knees. I went to the bureau and took out a pair of brown leather work gloves and slipped them on, slowly, like I'd seen Jack Palance do in *Shane*, wiggling my fingers down into them till they were snug.

"What is your name?" I said.

He gathered some saliva in his mouth and spit on the rug in my direction.

I took two steps toward him, grabbed hold of his chin with my left hand and yanked his face up at mine. He took a gravity knife out of his sock and made a pass at my throat. I leaned back and the point just nicked me under the chin. I caught the knife hand at the wrist as it went by with my right, stepped around behind him, put my left hand into his armpit and dislocated his elbow. The knife fell to the carpet. He made a harsh, half-stifled yell.

I kicked the knife across the room and let go of his arm. It hung at an odd angle. I stepped away from him and went to look at my chin in the mirror over the bureau. There was already blood all over my chin and dripping on my shirt. I took a clean handkerchief from the drawer and blotted up enough of the blood to see that the cut was minor, little more than a razor nick, maybe an inch long. I folded the handkerchief over and held it against the cut.

"Sloppy frisk," I said. "My own fault, Suck."

He sat still in the chair, his face tight and pale with pain.

"When you tell me what I want to know I'll get a doctor. What's your name?"

"Up your bleeding ass."

"I could do the other arm the same."

He was silent.

"Or the same one again."

"I am not going to say nothing," he said, his voice strained and shallow as he held against the pain. "No matter what you do. No bloody red sucking Yankee thug is going to make me say anything I don't want."

I took my Identikit sketches out and looked at them. He could have been one of them. I couldn't be sure. Dixon would have to ID him. I put the sketches away, took out the card that Downes had given me, went over to the phone and called him.

"I guess I got another one, Inspector. Fat little guy with blond hair and a Colt .22 target pistol."

"Are you at your hotel?"

"Yes, sir."

"I'll come over there, then."

"Yes, sir, and he needs a doctor. I had to bend his arm some."

"I'll call the hotel and have their man sent up."

The doctor arrived about five minutes before Downes did. It was Kensy, same doctor who'd been in to treat me. Today he had on a three-piece gray worsted suit with the waist nipped in and a lot of shoulder padding and a black silk shirt with long collar rolled out over the lapels.

"Well, sir," he said as he came in, "how's your arse?" And put his head back and laughed.

"What do you wear in surgery," I said, "a hot pink surgical mask?"

"My dear man, I don't do surgery. I'd better have a look at that chin though."

"Nope, just look at this guy's arm," I said.

He knelt beside the chair and looked at the kid's arm.

"Dislocated," he said. "Have to go to a hospital to have it set." He looked at me. "You do this?"

I nodded. "You're quite a lethal chap, aren't you?" he said.

"My entire body is a dangerous weapon," I said.

"Mm, I would think so," he said. "I'll put a kind of splint on that, my man," he said to the kid, "and give you something for the pain. And then we'd best bundle you off to the hospital and have an orthopedic man deal with it. I gather you have to wait on the authorities, however."

The kid didn't speak. "Yeah, he has to do that," I said.

Kensy took an inflatable splint from his bag and very gently put it onto the kid's damaged arm. Then he blew it up. He filled a hypodermic needle and gave him a shot. "You should feel better," he said, "in just a minute."

Kensy was putting the needle back in the bag when Downes came in. He looked at the kid with his arm in the temporary cast that looked like a transparent balloon. "Another half a car, Spenser?"

"Maybe. I think so, but it's hard to be sure."

There was a uniformed cop and a young woman in civilian clothes with Downes. "Tell me about this one," Downes said. The young woman sat down and took out a notebook. The uniformed bobby stood by the door. Kensy had his bag closed and headed for the door.

"That's only a temporary cast," he said to Downes. "Best get him prompt orthopedic attention."

"We'll get him to the hospital straight away," Downes said. "Fifteen minutes, no more."

"Good," Kensy said. "Try to avoid hurting anyone for a day or two, would you, Spenser. I'm going on holiday tonight, and I won't be back until Monday."

"Have a nice time," I said.

He left.

"Can you hold him for Dixon to look at?" I said.

"I imagine we can. What charges are you suggesting?"

"Oh, what, possession of a stolen weapon, possession of an unlicensed weapon, assault."

"You assaulted me, you red sucking son of a bitch," he said.

"Using profanity in front of a police officer," I said.

"We'll find an appropriate charge," Downes said. "Right now I'd like to hear the story."

I told him. The young lady wrote down everything we said.

"And the other one ran off on you," Downes said. "Unfortunate. You'd have had the start, perhaps, on another car."

"I could have killed him," I said.

"I am aware of that, Spenser. It's one reason I am not pressing you harder about all this." He looked at the bobby. "Gates," he said. "Take this gentleman down to the car. Be careful of his arm. I'll be right along and we'll take him to the hospital. Murray," he said to the young lady, "you go along with them."

The three of them left. The kid never looked at me. I was still holding the handkerchief to my chin. "You ought to clean that up and get a bandage on it," Downes said.

"I will in a minute," I said.

"Yes, well, I have two things I wish to say, Spenser. One, I would get some help, were I you. They've tried twice in two days. There's no reason to think that they will not try again. I don't think this is a one-man job."

"I was thinking the same thing. I'll put in a call to the States tonight."

"That's the second thing I wish to say. I am ambivalent about this entire adventure. So far you have probably done the British government and the city of London a favor by taking three terrorists out of circulation. I appreciate that. But I am not comfortable about an armed counterinsurgency movement developing in my city, conducted by Americans who operate without very much concern for British law or indeed for British custom. If you must import help, I will not allow an army of hired thugs to run loose in my city shooting terrorists on sight, and, in passing, making my department look rather bad."

"No sweat, Downes. If I get help it will be just one guy, and we'll stay out of the papers."

"You hope to stay out of the papers. But it will not be easy. The *Evening Standard* and the *Evening News* have been very insistent on getting the story of last night's shooting. I've put them off but inevitably someone will give them your name.''

''I don't want ink,'' I said. ''I'll shoot them away.''

''I hope so,'' Downes said. ''I hope too that you'll not be staying with us a great many more days, hmm?''

''We'll see,'' I said.

''Yes,'' Downes said. ''Of course we will.''

11

I sat on the bed and read the dialing instructions on the phone. I was exhausted. It was hard even to read the instructions. I had to run through them twice before I figured out that by dialing a combination of area codes I could call Susan Silverman direct. I tried it. The first time nothing happened. The second time I got a recorded message that I had screwed up. The third time it worked. The wires hummed a little bit, relays clicked in beneath the hum, a sound of distance and electricity hovered in the background, and then the phone rang and Susan answered, sounding just as she did. Mr. Watson, come here, I need you.

"It's your darling," I said.

"Which one," she said.

"Don't be a smartass," I said.

"Where are you?" she said.

"Still in London. I just dialed a few numbers and here we are."

"Oh, I had hoped you were at the airport wanting a ride home."

"Not yet, lovey," I said. "I called for two reasons. One to say that I love your ass. And second, to ask you to do me a service."

"Over the phone?"

"Not that kind of service," I said. "I want you to make a phone call for me. Got a pencil?"

"Just a minute . . . okay."

"Call Henry Cimoli"—I spelled it—"at the Harbor Health Club in Boston. It's in the book. Tell him to get hold of Hawk and tell Hawk I've got work for him over here. You got that so far?"

"Yes."

"Tell him to get the first plane he can to London and call me at the Mayfair Hotel when he gets to Heathrow."

"Mm hmm."

"Tell him money is no problem. He can name his price. But I want him now. Or sooner."

"It's bad," Susan said.

"What's bad?"

"Whatever you're doing. I know Hawk, I know what he's good at. If you need him it means that it's bad."

"No, not too bad. I need him to see that it doesn't get bad. I'm okay, but tell Henry to make sure that Hawk gets here. I don't want Hawk to come to the hotel. I want him to call me from Heathrow, and I'll get to him. Okay?"

"Okay. Who is Henry Cimoli?"

"He's like the pro at the Harbor Health Club. Little guy, used to fight. Pound for pound he's probably the strongest man I know. Before it got fancy, the Harbor Health Club used to be a gym. Hawk and I both trained there when we were fighting. Henry sort of trained us. He'll know where Hawk is."

"I gather you don't have Hawk's address. I would be willing to talk with him direct."

"I know you would. But Hawk doesn't have an address. He lives mostly with women, and between women he lives in hotels."

"What if he won't come?"

"He'll come."

"How can you be sure?"

"He'll come," I said. "How's Techniques of Counseling doing?"

"Fine, I got an A— on the midterm."

"Minus," I said. "That sonovabitch. When I come home I want his address."

"First thing?"

"No."

There was a small pause.

"It's hard on the phone," I said.

"I know. It's hard at long distance in any event. And . . . it's like having someone in the war. I don't like you sending for Hawk."

"It's just to help me do surveillance. Even Lord Peter Wimsey has to whiz occasionally."

Susan's laugh across the ocean, only slightly distorted by distance, made me want to cry. "I believe," she said. "that Lord Peter's butler does it for him."

"When this is over maybe you and I can come," I said. "It should be very fine for you and me to go around and look at the sights and maybe up to Stratford or down to Stonehenge. London gives me that feeling, you know. That excited feeling, like New York."

"If a man tires of London, he is tired of life," Susan said.

"Would you come over?"

"When?"

"Whenever I'm through. I'll send you some of my profits and meet you here. Would you come?"

"Yes," she said.

There was another small pause.

"We'd better hang up," she said. "This must be costing a great deal of money."

"Yeah, okay. It's Dixon's money, but there's not much else to say. I'll call tomorrow at this same time to see if Henry got Hawk. Okay?"

"Yes, I'll be home."

"Okay. I love you, Suze."

"Love."

"Goodbye."

"Goodbye." She hung up and I listened to the transoceanic buzz for a minute. Then I put the phone down, leaned back on the bed, and fell asleep fully dressed with the lights on and my folded handkerchief still pressed against my chin.

When I woke up in the morning the dried blood made the handkerchief, now unfurled, stick to my chin, and the first thing I had to do when I got up was to soak it off in cold water in the sink in the bathroom.

Getting the handkerchief off started the cut bleeding again, and I got a butterfly bandage out of my bag and put it on. I showered even more carefully than yesterday, keeping the water off both bandages. Not easy. If they kept after me in a while I'd have to start going dirty. I shaved around the new cut and toweled off. I changed the dressing on my bullet wound, turning half around and watching in the mirror to do it. There didn't seem to be any infection. I bundled last night's clothes into a laundry bag and left it for the hotel laundry. My shirt was a mess. I didn't have much hope for it. If I stayed here long enough they'd probably hire a blood removal specialist.

I had juice, oatmeal and coffee for breakfast, and went back out to watch my suspect. It was raining and I put on my light beige trench coat. I didn't have a hat but there was a shop on Berkeley Street and I bought one of those Irish walking hats. Me and Pat Moynihan. When I got home I could wear it to the Harvard Club. They'd think I was faculty. With the hat turned down over my eyes and my trench coat collar up I wasn't terribly recognizable. But I was terribly silly-looking. The broken nose and the scar tissue around the eyes somehow didn't go with the Eton and Harrow look.

It was a pleasant rain and I didn't mind walking in it. In fact I liked it. Come on with the rain, there's a smile on my face. I varied my route, going east on Piccadilly and Shaftesbury and up Charing Cross and Tottenham Court Road. All the way I kept an eye out for a tail, doubling back on my route a couple of times. I came in Tottenham Street to her apartment building staying close to the wall. The only way she could see me was if she stuck her head out the window and looked straight down. If anyone was following me they were very goddamned good.

I turned into her apartment house doorway and looked in the foyer. There were three apartments. Two were Mr. and Mrs. One was simply K. CALDWELL. I was betting on K. Caldwell.

I rang the bell. Over the intercom a voice, distorted by the cheap equipment but recognizably female, said, "Yes?"

"Mr. Western?" I said, reading the name above Caldwell's.

"Who?"

"Mr. Western."

"You've pushed the wrong button, mate. He lives upstairs." The intercom went dead. I went out of the foyer and across the street and by the hospital, underneath an overhang, and waited concealed by some shrubbery. Shortly before noon she came out and headed up Cleveland Street. She turned right on Howland and was out of sight. I waited five minutes. She didn't reappear. I walked across to the foyer again and rang the bell under K. CALDWELL.

No answer. I rang it again and kept my thumb on it. No one.

The front door to the building wasn't even locked. I went in and up to the second floor. Her door was locked. I knocked. No answer. I got out my small lock picker and went to work. I'd made the lock picker myself. It looked a little like a buttonhook made of thin stiff wire, and it had a small L on the tip. The idea was to slip it into the keyhole and then one by one turn the tumbler, working by feel. Some locks if you got it in one of the tumbler slots all the tumblers would turn at once. Sometimes, in better locks, you had to turn several. K. Caldwell did not have a good lock. It took about thirty-five seconds to get her apartment door open. I stepped in. It was empty. There's a feel to a place almost as soon as you step in that says if it's empty or not. I was rarely wrong about that. Still, I took my gun out and walked through the place.

It looked as if it were ready for inspection.

Everything was immaculate. The living room was furnished in angular plastic and stainless steel. On one wall was a bookcase with books in several languages. The books were perfectly organized. Not by language or topic, but by size, highest books in the center, smallest at each end, so that the shelves were symmetrical. Most of the books I'd never heard of, but I recognized Hobbes, and *Mein Kampf*. There were four magazines stacked on the near right-hand corner of the coffee table. The one on top was in a Scandinavian language. The title was spelled with one of those little o's with a slash through it. Like in Søren Kierkegaard. On the far left-hand corner was crystal sculpture that looked sort of like a water jet, frozen. In the center, exactly between the magazines and the crystal, was a round stainless steel ashtray with no trace of ash in it.

I moved to the bedroom. It too was furnished in early

Bauhaus. The bedspread was white and drawn so tight across the bed that a quarter probably would have bounced on it. There were three Mondrian prints in stainless steel frames on the white walls. One on each. The fourth wall was broken by the window. Everything in the room was white except the Mondrians and a steel-gray rug on the floor.

I opened the closet. There were skirts and blouses and dresses and slacks precisely folded and creased and hung in careful groupings on hangers. The clothes were all gray or white or black. On the shelf were six pairs of shoes in order. There was nothing else in the closet. The bathroom was entirely white except the shower curtain, which was black with silver squares on it. The toothpaste tube on the sink was neatly rolled up from the bottom. The water glass was clean. In the medicine cabinet was underarm deodorant, a safety razor, a comb, a brush, a container of dental floss, a bottle of castor oil, and a can of feminine deodorant spray. No sign of make-up.

I went back in the bedroom and began to go through the bureau. The top two drawers contained sweaters and blouses, gray, black, white and one beige. The bottom drawer was locked. I picked the lock and opened it. It contained underwear. Perhaps twelve pairs of French string bikini underpants in lavender, cerise, emerald, peach and flowered patterns. There were bras in 36C that matched the underpants. Most of them trimmed with lace, and diaphanous. There was a black lace garter belt and three pairs of black fishnet stockings. I thought pantyhose had put the garter belt people out of business. There was also a collection of perfume and a negligee.

The drawer was heavy. I measured the inside roughly with my hand span. Then I did the outside. The outside was about a hand span deeper. I felt the inside bottom of the drawer all around the edge. At one spot it gave, and when I pressed it the bottom tilted. I lifted it out and there were four guns, .22 caliber target pistols, and ten boxes of ammunition. There were six hand grenades of a type I hadn't seen. There was also a notebook with lists of names I'd never heard of, and addresses next to them. There were four passports. All with the girl's picture on them. One Canadian, one Danish, one British, one Dutch. Each one had a different name. I copied them into my notebook. The British one had the name Katherine Caldwell. There were a couple of letters in the Scandinavian language full of o's, and one bayonet that said U.S. on it. The letters were postmarked in Amsterdam. I took down the address. I looked at the list of names. It was too long to copy. The addresses were street addresses without cities attached, but obviously some were not English, and, as far as I could tell, none was American. My name wasn't on the list.

Neither was Dixon's. It could be a list of victims, or a list of safe houses, or a list of Liberty recruits, or a list of people who'd sent her Christmas cards last winter. I put the false bottom back in the drawer and slid it back and locked it.

The rest of the house didn't tell me much else. I found out that Katherine was into bran cereal and fruit juices. That she dusted under the bed and behind the sofa, and that she owned neither television nor radio. Probably spent her free time reading *Leviathan* and breaking bricks with the edge of her hand.

12

I was back out in the street by the hospital behind my shrub in the rain when Katherine returned. Her real name was probably none of the four, but Katherine was the easiest one so I called her that. Having a name made her easier to think about.

She was wearing a white belted raincoat and carrying a transparent plastic umbrella that had a deep bow so that she was able to protect her whole head and shoulders. There were black slacks and black boots showing under the raincoat. I speculated on the undies. Hot pink perhaps? She went in her apartment and didn't come out again. No one else went in. I stood in the rain for three more hours. My feet were very wet and very tired of being stood on. I walked back to the Mayfair.

That night I made a sixty-three-dollar phone call to Susan. The first dollar's worth told me that Henry had got in touch with Hawk and Hawk would be over right away. The next sixty-two dollars were about who missed who and what we'd do and see when she came over. There was some brief talk about whether anyone was going to do me in. I maintained that no one was, and Susan said she hoped I was right. I thought I wouldn't mention my wounds right then.

I hung up feeling worse than I had for a while. Talking

on the phone from 5000 miles away was like the myth of Tantalus. It was better not to. The telephone company has lied to us for years, I thought. Always tell you that long distance is the next best thing to being there. All those people call up and feel swell afterward. I didn't. I felt like beating up a nun.

I had room service bring up some beer and sandwiches and I sat in my chair by the airshaft and read *Regeneration Through Violence* and ate sandwiches and drank beer for nearly four hours. Then I went to bed and slept.

Hawk didn't make it the next day, and I didn't either. Katherine stayed in her apartment all day, modeling her lingerie and spraying herself with deodorant or whatever she did. I stayed outside in the rain modeling my walking hat and trench coat and listening to my shoes squish. No urban guerrillas appeared. No one went in or out of the apartment building that looked even vaguely like he might carry a knuckle knife. The rain was hard and steady and persistent. No one wanted to be out in it. There was little movement on Katherine's street, almost none in or out of her building. From where I stood I could see the call buttons in the foyer. No one pushed hers. I spent my time figuring out the time sequence for Hawk's likely arrival. To expect him today was cutting it too close. Tomorrow he'd come. I kept adding and subtracting six hours to all my calculations until my head began to hurt and I thought about other things.

Interesting girl, old Katherine. Everything black and white and stainless steel. Spotless and deodorized and exactly symmetrical and a drawer full of peepshow underwear. Times Square sexy. Repression. Maybe I should pick up a copy of Krafft-Ebing on my way back to the Mayfair. Then I could call up Susan and have her explain it to me. While I stood, I ate a Hershey bar with almonds, and a green apple. Lunch. I don't remember James Bond doing this, I thought. He was always having stone crab and pink champagne. I called it quits at dinner time and went back to the Mayfair, did a repeat of the previous evening. High adventure in swinging London. I was in bed before ten.

In the morning I followed Katherine to the Reading Room in the British Museum. She got a desk and began to read. I stood around outside in the entry foyer and looked into the enormous high-domed room. There was a grand and august quality about it all. It looked like one thought it would. Lots of places don't. Times Square, for instance. Or Piccadilly, for that matter. But when I'd first seen Stonehenge it was everything it should have been, and so was the British Museum. I could imagine Karl Marx writing the *Communist Manifesto* there, hunched over one of the desks in the whispering semi-silence beneath the enormous dome. At noon she came out of the Reading Room and went to have lunch in the small cafeteria downstairs beyond the Mausoleum Room. When she was seated, I left her and went back to call the hotel.

"Yes, sir, there is a message for you," the clerk said. "A Mr. Stepinfetchit is waiting for you near the Pan American ticket counter at Heathrow Airport." There was nothing incorrect in the clerk's voice, and if the name struck him as odd he didn't let on.

"Thank you," I said. Time to leave Katherine and go get Hawk. I got a cab on Great Russell Street and rode out to the airport. Hawk was easy to spot if you knew what you were looking for. I saw him leaning back in a chair with his feet on a suitcase and a white straw hat with a lavender band and a broad brim tipped forward over his face. He had on a dark blue three-piece suit, with a fine pinstripe of light gray, a white shirt with a collar pin underneath the small tight four-in-hand knot of a lavender silk tie. The points of a lavender handkerchief showed in his breast pocket. His black over-the-ankle boots gleamed with wax. The suitcase on which they rested must have cost half a grand. Hawk was stylish.

I said, "Excuse me, Mr. Fetchit, I've seen all your movies and was wondering if you'd care to join me for a bite of watermelon."

Hawk didn't move. His voice came from under the hat, "Y'all can call me Stepin, bawse."

The seat next to him was empty. I sat down beside him. "I'm sorry," I said, "things must be going bad for you, Hawk, having to wear that rag over here and all."

"Boy, I brought this last time I was here. Bond Street. The man fitted it right to my body." He took his hat off and held it in his lap while he looked at me. He was completely bald and his black skin glistened in the airport fluorescence. Everything fitted Hawk well. His skin was smooth and tight over his face and skull. The cheekbones were high and prominent.

"You got a gun," I said.

He shook his head. "I didn't want no hassle at the customs. You know I got no license."

"Yeah, okay. I can supply one. How you feel about a Colt .22 target pistol?"

Hawk looked at me. "What you doing with that trash? You showing off how good you are?"

"Nope, I took it off somebody."

Hawk shrugged. "It's better than nothing, till I can accumulate something better. What you into?"

I told him I was bounty-hunting.

"Twenty-five hundred a head," he said. "How much of that is mine?"

"None, you're overhead. I'll pay a hundred fifty a day and expenses, and bill it to Dixon."

Hawk shrugged. "Okay."

I gave him 500 pounds. "Get a room at the Mayfair. Pretend you don't know me. They are trying to tail me and if they see us together they'll know you too." I gave him my room number. "You can call me after you've checked in and we'll get together."

"How you know they didn't tail you out here and spot us together, old buddy?"

I scowled at him. "Are you kidding," I said.

"O yeah, tha's you, babe, Mr. Humble."

"Nobody tailed me. These people are dangerous but they are amateurs," I said.

"And you and me ain't," Hawk said. "We surely ain't."

An hour later, I was back at my room at the Mayfair waiting for Hawk to call. When he did, I got one of the .22 target pistols I'd taken from the assassins and went down to see him. He was four floors below me but I went up and down and on and off the elevator a few times to make sure I didn't have a tail.

Hawk was in his underwear, hanging up his clothes very carefully and sipping champagne from a tall tulip-shaped glass. His shorts were lavender-colored silk. I took the .22 out of the waist band of my pants and put it on the table.

"I see you've already found the room service number," I said.

"I surely have. There's some beer in the bathroom sink." Hawk rehung a pair of pearl gray slacks on a hanger so that the creases in each pant leg were exactly even. I went into the bathroom. Hawk had filled the sink with ice and put six bottles of Amstel beer and another bottle of Taittinger champagne in to chill. I opened a beer on the bottle opener by the bathroom door and stepped back into the bedroom. Hawk had the clip out of the .22 I had brought and was checking the action. Shaking his head.

"The bad guys use these over here?"

"Not all the time," I said. "It's just what they could get."

Hawk shrugged and slipped the clip back in the butt. "Better than screaming for help," he said. I drank some beer. Amstel. No one imported it at home anymore. Fools.

Hawk said, "While I'm hanging up the vines, man, you might want to talk some more about why I'm here."

I did. I gave him everything, from the first time I'd met Hugh Dixon on the terrace in Weston, until this morning when I'd left Katherine sorting her French bikini undies and musing passionately about the teachings of Savonarola.

"Shit," Hawk said. "French bikinis. What she look like?"

"She's up to your standards, Hawk, but we've come to follow Katherine, not to screw her."

"Doing one don't mean you can't do the other."

"We'll threaten her with that when we want information," I said.

Hawk drank some more champagne. "You hungry?"

I nodded. I couldn't ever really remember when I hadn't been.

"I'll have them send up something," Hawk said. "How about a mess of shrimp cocktail?" He didn't bother to look at the room service menu on the bureau.

I nodded again. Hawk ordered. The first bottle of champagne was gone and he popped the cork on the second. He showed no sign that he'd drunk anything. In fact in the time I'd known Hawk I'd never seen him show a sign of anything. He laughed easily and he was never off balance.

But whatever went on inside stayed inside. Or maybe nothing went on inside. Hawk was as impassive and hard as an obsidian carving. Maybe that was what went on inside. He sipped some champagne.

"And you want me to keep your ass covered while you chase these crazies."

"Yes."

"What do we do with them when you catch them?"

"That's sort of up to them."

"You mean if they give us trouble we whack them out?"

"If we have to."

"Why not go the easy route and whack 'em out right off?"

I shook my head.

Hawk laughed. "Same old Spenser. You still go the hard way."

I shrugged and got another Amstel from the sink. The room service waiter arrived with the shrimp cocktail and I stayed in the bathroom out of sight until he was gone. When the door closed, Hawk said, "Okay, Spenser. I paid for it, you can come out."

"You can't tell who they have in their employ," I said. On the room service cart were ten shrimp cocktails, each in its individual ice dish, and two forks. Hawk ate a shrimp.

"Not bad," he said. "Okay. I can dig it. You paying the ace and half a day, you say how we do it."

I nodded again.

"What we going to do first?"

"We'll eat this shrimp and drink this beer and wine and go to sleep. Tomorrow morning I'm going to watch Katherine some more. I'll call you before I leave and you can cover me."

"Okay. Then what?"

"Then we'll see what happens."

"What happens if I pick up somebody tagging after you?"

"Just watch them. Don't let them shoot me."

"Do mah best." Hawk grinned, his teeth flawless and white in the glistening ebony face. "Long as I don't get too distracted by the lady with the French bikinis."

"You can probably bribe her with a pair of yours," I said.

13

We followed my plan for nearly a week. No one killed me. No one tried. Hawk drifted around behind me in $5000 worth of clothes earning his $150 a day. We saw nothing interesting. We spotted no one on my list of crazies. We stood around and watched Kathie's apartment and followed her to the British Museum and the grocery store.

"You scared them," Hawk said while we ate dinner in his room. "They sent their best people after you twice and you ate them alive. They scared. They laying low now."

"Yeah. They're not even watching me. Unless they are so good neither one of us has spotted them."

Hawk said, "Haw."

"Yeah. We'd have spotted them. You think Kathie has spotted me?"

Hawk shook his head.

"So they don't know if I'm still after them or not."

"Maybe check the hotel once in a while, see if you still registered."

"Yeah. They could do that," I said. "And they will just keep it cool till I leave."

"Or maybe they got nothing to keep cool," Hawk said.

"Yeah, it may not be all that organized anyway and there's nothing in the works whether I'm here or not."

"Maybe."

"Could be. I'm getting sick of waiting around. Let's put some pressure on old Kath."

"I can dig that."

"Not that kind of pressure, Hawk. I'll let her spot me. If she gets scared maybe she'll run. If she runs maybe we can follow her and find some people."

"And when she runs I'll be behind her," Hawk said. "She'll think she lost you."

"Yeah. Keep in mind that these people aren't necessarily English. If she bolts she may head for another country and you better be ready."

"I am always ready, my man. Whatever I'm wearing is home."

"That's another thing," I said. "Try not to wear your shellpink jumpsuit when you tail her. Sometimes people notice things like that. I know that's your idea of inconspicuous, but . . ."

"You ever hear of me losing somebody or getting spotted by someone I didn't want to spot me?"

"Just a suggestion. I am, after all, your employer."

"Yowsah boss, y'all awful kind to hep ol Hawk lak yew do."

"Why don't you can that Aunt Jemima crap," I said. "You're about as down-home darkie as Truman Capote."

Hawk sipped some champagne, and put the glass down. He sliced a small portion of Scottish smoked salmon and ate it. He drank some more champagne.

"Just a poor old colored person," he said. "Trying to get along with the white folks."

"Well, I'll give you credit, you were one of the first to integrate leg-breaking on an interracial basis in Boston."

"A man is poor indeed if he don't do something for his people."

"Who the hell are your people, Hawk?"

"Those good folks regardless of race, creed or color, who have the coin to pay me."

"You ever think about being black, Hawk?"

He looked at me for maybe ten seconds. "We a lot alike, Spenser. You got more scruples maybe, but we alike. Except one thing. You never been black. That's something I know that you won't ever know."

"So you do think about it. How is it?"

"I used to think about it, when I had to. I don't have to no more. Now I ain't nigger any more than you honkie. Now I drink the wine and screw the broads and take the money and nobody shoves me. Now I just play all the time. And the games I play nobody can play as good." He drank some more champagne, his movements clean and sure and delicate. He was eating with no shirt on and the overhead light made the planes of muscle cast fluid and intricate highlights on the black skin. He put the champagne glass back on the table, cut another slice of salmon and stopped with the portion halfway to his mouth. He looked at me again and his face opened into a brilliant, oddly mirthless grin. " 'Cept maybe you, babe," he said.

"Yeah," I said, "but the game's not the same."

Hawk shrugged. "Same game, different rules."

"Maybe," I said. "I never been sure you had any rules."

"You know better. I just got fewer than you. And I ain't softhearted. But you know, I say I gonna do something I do it. It gets done. I hire on for something, I stay hired. I do what I take the bread for."

"I remember a time you didn't stay hired for King Powers."

"That's different," Hawk said. "King Powers is a douche bag. He got no rules, he don't count. I mean you, or

Henry Cimoli. I tell you something, you can put it in the bank.''

"Yeah. That's so," I said. "Who else?" Hawk had drunk a lot of Taittinger and I had drunk a lot of Amstel.

"Who else what?"

"Who else can trust you?"

"Quirk," Hawk said.

"Martin Quirk," I said. "Detective Lieutenant Martin Quirk?"

"Yeah."

"Quirk wants to put you in the joint."

"Sure he does," Hawk said. "But he knows how a man acts. He knows how to treat a man."

"Yeah, you're right. Anyone else?"

"That's enough. You, Henry, Quirk. That's more than a lot of people ever know."

"I don't guess Henry will give you trouble," I said. "But Quirk or I may shoot you someday."

Hawk finished his salmon and turned the big bright grin at me again. "If you can, man. If you can."

Hawk pushed the plate away, and stood up. "Got something to show you," he said.

I sipped at my beer while he went to the closet and brought out something that looked like a cross between a shoulder holster and a backpack. He slipped his arms through the loops and stepped back from the closet. "What do you think?"

The rig was a shoulder holster for a sawed-off shotgun. The straps went around each shoulder and the gun hung, butt down along his spine.

"Watch this," he said. He slipped his coat on over his naked skin. The coat covered the gun entirely. Unless you were looking you didn't even see a bulge. With his right hand he reached behind him under the skirt of his suit jacket, gave a brief twisting movement and brought the shotgun out.

"Can you dig it?"

"Lemme see," I said. And Hawk put the shotgun in my hand. It was an Ithaca double-barreled 12 gauge. The stock had been cut off and both barrels were cut back. The whole thing was no more than eighteen inches long. "Do a lot more damage than a target pistol," I said.

"And it's no problem. Just go buy a shotgun and cut it down. If we have to go to another country I ditch this and buy a new one where we going. Take me an hour maybe to modify the mother."

"Got a hack saw?"

Hawk nodded. "And a couple of C clamps. That's all I need."

"Not bad," I said. "What you going to do next, modify an Atlas missile and walk around with it tucked in your sock?"

"No harm," Hawk said, "to fire power."

The next morning I got up early and went up and burgled Kathie's apartment while she was at the laundromat. I was neat about it, but sloppy enough to let her know someone had been there. I wasn't looking for anything, I just wanted her to know someone had been there. I was in and out in about five minutes. When she came back I was leaning in the doorway of the next apartment house wearing sunglasses. As she passed I turned away so she wouldn't see my face. I wanted her to spot me but I didn't want to overact.

I used to know a guy named Shelley Walden when I was with the cops who would get spotted tailing a guy through a rock concert. I never knew why he was so bad at it. He had a small, innocuous look about him and he wasn't clumsy, but he couldn't keep out of sight. I tried to run this stakeout like Shelley would have.

If she spotted me when she went by she didn't let on. I knew Hawk was somewhere behind her but I didn't see him. When she went into her apartment I walked casually across the street and leaned on a lamppost and took out a newspaper and started to read it. That would have been Shelley's style. The old Bogart movies where he pulls back the curtain and there's a guy under a lamppost reading a newspaper. I figured she'd see that someone had been rummaging in her apartment and that would get her nervous. It did.

About two minutes after she went in, I saw her looking out her window. I was looking surreptitiously over my newspaper and for a moment our eyes met. I looked back down at the newspaper. She knew I was there. She should recognize me. It was sunny and I wasn't wearing my Irish walking hat. No mistaking me for Rex Harrison.

She had reason to be nervous about being spotted. She had phony passports and stolen guns in her bedroom. That would be enough to bust her. But I wanted them all. She was the string and they were the balloon. If I cut her off I lost the balloon. She was all the handle I had.

What she should have done was sit tight, but she didn't know that. She would either call out the shooters again, or she'd run. She sat in her apartment and looked at me looking at her for nearly four hours, and then she ran. Hawk had been right. The shooters must be getting wary of me. Or maybe I'd cleaned them out. Maybe all the shooters the organization had had been used up, except the one guy that got away. I wasn't dealing here with the KGB. Liberty's resources were probably limited.

She came out of her apartment at about two in the afternoon. She was wearing a tan safari jacket and matching pants and carrying a very large shoulder bag. The same one she'd had at the zoo. She was careful not to pay me any attention as she went past me on Cleveland and headed up Goodge Street toward Bloomsbury. For a half hour it was hare and hounds with Kathie dekeing and diving the side streets of Bloomsbury with me behind her and Hawk behind me. At every turn I kept before me the clear image of Shelley Walden. When in doubt I asked myself, "What would Shelley do?" Everywhere she went, she saw me behind her. Only once in all of this did I catch sight of Hawk. He was in Levis and a corduroy sport coat, surprisingly innocuous, on the opposite side of the street going the other way.

I let her lose me in the Russell Square Underground. She got on and I got on. At the last minute she got off and I let her go. As the train pulled out she was heading back out of the station and, behind her, Hawk, with his hands in his hip pockets and the faint bulge of the shotgun along his spine. He was smiling as the train went into the tunnel.

14

I went back and staked out Kathie's apartment, but she never came back. Good. She was probably headed for a new place. Any pattern break was better than none at this point. After dinner that night I finished up *Regeneration Through Violence* and was thumbing through the *International Herald Tribune* when Hawk called.

"Where are you?" I said.

"Copenhagen, babe, the Paris of the North."

"Where is she?"

"She here too. She checked into an apartment here. You coming over?"

"Yeah. Be there tomorrow. Anyone with her?"

"Not yet. She just flew over, came to the apartment and went in. She ain't come out."

"The revolutionaries do lead an exciting life, don't they?"

"Like you and me, babe, international adventurers. I'm at the Sheraton Copenhagen watching Danish television. What you doing, man?"

"I was glancing through the *Herald Tribune* when you called. Very interesting. An enriching experience."

Hawk said, "Yeah. Me too."

"I'll come over tomorrow," I said.

"Room five-two-three," Hawk said. "Have them pack

up my stuff and ship it to Henry. Hate to have some limey walking around in my threads."

"Ah Hawk," I said, "you sentimental bastard."

"You gonna like it here, babe," Hawk said.

"Why is that?"

"The broads are all blond and they sell beer in the Coke machine."

"Maybe I'll come over tonight," I said. But I didn't. I slept another night in England. In the morning I arranged for Hawk's stuff to be shipped to the States. I called Flanders and told him where I was going. Then I packed my gun as before, in my luggage, and flew to Denmark. Have gun, will travel. Did Paladin do vengeance? Probably.

The airport at Copenhagen was modern and glassy, with a lot of level escalators to move people around the airport. I took a bus in from the airport to the SAS terminal in the Royal Hotel. On the way I spotted the Sheraton. A short walk from the terminal. I made the walk carrying my flight bag, my suitcase and my garment bag, feeling the odd excited buzz I always felt in a place I'd never been.

The Sheraton looked like Sheratons I'd seen in New York, Boston and Chicago. Newer maybe than New York and Chicago. More like Boston. It looked as Danish as Bond bread. I checked in. The desk clerk spoke English with no accent. Embarrassing. I didn't even know how to say Søren Kierkegaard. The hell with him. How many one-armed push-ups can he do?

I unpacked and dialed room 523. No answer. The air conditioner was purring under the window but wasn't cooling the room. The temperature was about 96. I opened the windows and looked out. There was a broad park across the street with a lake in it. The park extended several blocks down to the right. Across the park I could see another hotel. The open window's help was largely psychological, but I didn't feel quite as bad. I reassembled my gun, loaded it, put it in its shoulder holster and hung the rig on a chair back. My shirt was wet. I took it off. The rest of me was wet too. I took off my clothes, brought the gun and holster with me into the bathroom, hung it on the door knob and took a shower. Then I toweled off, put on clean clothes and looked out the window some more.

About two in the afternoon there was a knock on the door. I took my gun out, stood to one side of the door and said, "Yeah."

"Hawk."

I opened the door and he came in. He was wearing white Nikes with a red slash, and white duck pants and an off-white safari jacket with short sleeves. He was carrying two open bottles of Carlsberg beer.

"Fresh from the machine," he said, and gave me one.

I drank most of it. "I thought Scandinavia was cool and northern," I said.

"Heat wave," Hawk said. "Never had one like this before, they keep saying. That's why the air conditioners don't do shit. They never really use them."

I finished the beer. "Right in the Coke machine, you say?"

"Yeah, man, right on your floor here, around the corner from the elevator. You got any kroner?"

I nodded. "I exchanged some at the desk when I checked in."

"Come on, we'll get us a couple more. Helps with the heat."

We went out and got two more beers and came back in.

"Okay, where is she?" I said. The beer was very cool in my throat.

"About a block down that way," Hawk said. "You

lean far enough out your window, you probably see her place.''

"Why aren't you poised outside watching her every move?''

"She went in about eleven, nothing happened since. I was thirsty and I figured I'd come see if you got in.''

"Anything shaking since I talked with you before?''

"Naw. She hasn't done a thing. Somebody else staking her out though.''

"Ah hah," I said.

"What you say?''

"I said, Ah hah.''

"That what I thought you say. You honkies do talk strange.''

"They spot you?" I said.

"Course they didn't spot me. Would they spot you?''

"No. I withdraw the question.''

"Damn right.''

"What can you tell me about him?''

"Dark fella. Not a brother. Maybe a Syrian, something, some kind of Arab.''

"Tough?''

"Oh yeah. He got a look. I think he had a piece. Saw him sort of shrug like the shoulder holster straps was aggravating him.''

"How big?''

"Tall, taller than me. Not too heavy, sort of stoop-shouldered. Big beaky nose. Thirty, maybe thirty-five years old, crew-cut.''

I had out my descriptions and my Identikit drawings.

"Yeah," I said. "He's one.''

"Why is he watching her?" Hawk said.

"Maybe he's not watching her, maybe he's looking for me," I said.

"Yeah," Hawk said. "That's why she don't do much. Since I tailed her over she just take a couple walks, and come back. Each time the dude with the big honker he follow her, very loose. He stay back of her. He looking for you, see if she was followed."

I nodded. "Okay," I said. "She's got some people here. We'll play their match. I'll watch her. I'll let Big Nose watch me, and you can watch him. Then we'll see what happens."

"Maybe Big Nose burn you the first time he see you."

"You're not supposed to let him do that."

"Yeah."

The beer was gone. I looked at the empty bottle with sadness.

"Let's get to it," I said. "Sooner we get them all, the sooner I get home."

"You don't like foreigners?"

"I miss Susan."

"Can't blame you for that, man, she got one of the finest ass . . ."

I looked up.

Hawk said, "Cancel that, man. I sorry. That ain't your kind of talk about Susan. It ain't mine either. I forgot myself."

I nodded.

15

I went out of the Sheraton and turned left on Vester Søgade.
Most of the buildings along the street were low apartment
buildings, relatively new, and middle-class or better.
Number 36 was hers. Brick, with a small open porch on
the front. Before I got there I crossed the street and
lingered inconspicuously near some bushes in the park. A
lot of people must walk their dogs, I noticed, along a
narrow path that skirted the lake. A light blue Simca
cruised by with one man at the wheel. I stayed where I
was. I didn't see Hawk. In a few minutes the Simca was
back. A little one, square and boxy. It went past me going
the other way and parked a half block up toward the hotel.
I stood. It sat.

After another ten minutes a black Saab station wagon
pulled up in front of Kathie's apartment. Three men got
out and two of them began to walk toward me, the third
went into Kathie's. I looked in the other direction toward
the Simca. A tall, dark, stoop-shouldered man with a big
nose and a gray crew-cut was getting out. Behind me was
the lake. One of us was sort of cornered. The two men
from the Saab fanned out a little as they came so that if I
had wanted to I couldn't run straight ahead and split the
defense and get away. I didn't want to. I stood still with
my feet about a foot apart, my hands clasped loosely in

front of me, slightly below my belt buckle. The three men reached me and spread out in a little circle around me. The tall guy with the nose stood behind me.

The two men from the Saab looked like brothers. Young and ruddy-cheeked. One of them had a scar that ran from the corner of his mouth halfway across his cheek. The other had very small eyes and very light eyebrows. Both were wearing loud sport shirts hanging outside their pants. I guessed why. The one with the scar took a .38 automatic out of his waistband and pointed it at me. He said something in German.

"I speak English," I said.

"Put your hands on top of your head," he said.

"Wow," I said, "you hardly have an accent."

He gestured with the gun barrel. I rested my hands loosely on my head. "That seems dumb to me," I said. "Should ein cop come by he might notice that I was standing here with my hands on my head. He might pause to ask why, nein?"

"Put your hands down at your sides."

I put them down. "Which of you is Hans?"

The guy with the gun ignored me. He said something in German to the big-nosed guy behind me.

"I'll bet you're Hans," I said to Scarface. "And you're Fritz."

Big Nose patted me down, found my gun, and took it. He slipped it into his belt under his shirt. "That's the Captain behind me."

They didn't seem to be fans of the Katzenjammer Kids. They didn't seem to be fans of me either. The guy with the small eyes said, "Come." And we walked across the street from the park and into the apartment building. I was careful not to look for Hawk.

Kathie's apartment was first floor right, looking out on

the park. She was there when we went in, sitting on the couch, half turned so she could look out the window. She was wearing a white corduroy jumpsuit with a black chain for a belt. The man in the room with her was small and wiry with a wide, strong nose and a harsh mouth. He had a big gray mustache that extended beyond his lips, and he wore wire-rimmed glasses. He was nearly bald, probably, but he had let what little hair he had grow very long on the left side and then combed it up and across. Thus his part started just above his left ear. To keep it in place he seemed to have lacquered it with hair spray. He was wearing work shoes and tight-legged corduroy jeans. His white shirt was frayed at the collar. The sleeves were rolled up and his forearms looked strong. He was dark, like Big Nose, and middle-aged. He didn't look like a German, or a crazy. He looked like a mean grownup.

He spoke in German to Scarface.

Scarface said, "English."

"Why are you following this young woman?" the guy said to me. He had an accent, but I couldn't say what kind.

"Why do you want to know?" I said.

He took two steps across the room and punched me in the jaw with his right hand. He was a strong little man and the punch hurt. Hans and Fritz both had their guns out. Fritz's was a Luger. Big Nose stayed behind me.

"At least you gave me a straight answer," I said.

"Why are you following this young woman?"

"She and a number of her associates blew up the family of a rich and vengeful American," I said. "He hired me to get even."

"Then why did you simply not kill her when you found her?"

"One, I'm too nice a guy. Two, she was the only one I

had contact with. I wanted her for a Judas goat. I wanted her to lead me to the others.''

''And you think she has?''

''Some. You're new, but the guy with the big bazoo here and Hans and Fritz, they look about right.''

''How many people are involved?''

''Nine.''

''You have killed or captured three. You have located four more, and it has not taken you very long. You are good at your work.''

I tried to look modest.

''Someone that good at his work should not have been so easy to catch standing there in the park like a statue.''

I tried to look embarrassed.

''You were armed and you look dangerous. In the past you have killed two men lying in ambush for you.'' He looked out the window. ''Have we followed her down the slaughter chute as well?''

Big Nose said something in a language I didn't know. The little guy answered him. Big Nose went out the front door, moving with a kind of shambling lope.

''We shall see,'' the little guy said.

''What's your part in all of this?'' I said.

''I have the misfortune to have this collection of thugs and terrorists in my organization. I do not admire them. They are childish amateurs. I have business a good deal more serious to conduct than blowing up tourists in London. But I also have need of bodies and I cannot always choose the best.''

''It's hard to get good help,'' I said.

''It is that,'' he said. ''You would be good help, I think. I have knocked men down with punches no harder than I gave you.''

"You might try it sometime when your thugs and terrorists were not around to support you."

"I am not big, but I am quick and I know many tricks," he said. "But we're going to kill you so you and I will never know."

"You are when your friend Nose-o comes back and says there's no one waiting outside with an antitank gun."

The little guy smiled. "You are not an amateur either," he said. "We'll kill you whether there is someone there or not. But it is best to know. Perhaps you would serve as a hostage. We shall see."

"What's this important work you're doing?" I said.

"It is freedom's work. Africa does not belong to the Nigras or the Communists."

"Who does it belong to?"

"It belongs to us."

"Us?"

"You and me, the white race. The race that brought it out of the cesspool of tribalism and savagery in the nineteenth century. The race that can make Africa a civilization."

"You aren't Cecil Rhodes, are you?"

"My name is Paul."

"All your people share this goal?"

"We are prowhite and anticommunist," Paul said. "That is common ground enough."

"Let me ask you a question, Kathie," I said. "You speak English, I assume."

"I speak five languages," she said. She was on the couch in the same spot she'd been in when I came in. She was very still. When she spoke only her mouth moved.

"How do you wear white pants like that without the French bikinis showing through?"

Kathie's face turned a slow red. "You are filthy," she said.

Paul hit me again, with his left hand this time, evening up the bruises.

"Do not speak so to her," he said.

Kathie got up and left the room. Paul went after her. Hans and Fritz pointed their guns at me. A key turned in the door behind me and Big Nose stepped in.

"No one," he said. Hawk stepped in right behind him with two shotgun shells in his teeth and, firing past his ear with a cutdown shotgun, blew most of Fritz's head off. I dove behind a lounge chair. Hans fired at Hawk and hit Big Nose in the middle of the forehead. Hawk fired the second barrel at Hans as Big Nose was going down. It folded him over and he was dead by the time he fell. Hawk broke open the shotgun. The spent shells popped in the air. Hawk took the fresh shells from his mouth and slid them into the breech and snapped the shotgun closed by the time the spent shells hit the floor.

I was on my feet. "Through there," I said, and pointed toward the door where Kathie and Paul had left the room. Hawk reached it while I dug my gun out of Big Nose's belt.

"Door's locked," Hawk said.

I kicked it open and Hawk went through in a low crouch, the shotgun held in his right hand, and I went behind him. It was a bedroom and bath with sliding doors that opened onto a courtyard. The doors were open. Paul and Kathie were gone.

"Goddamn," Hawk said.

"Let's get the hell out of here," I said. We did.

16

The next morning we looked in the Danish papers. There was a front-page picture of Kathie's apartment and a shot of bodies being wheeled out on stretchers on page two. But neither Hawk nor I could read Danish so there wasn't much to learn. I clipped the story anyway, in case I found a translator. Hans and Fritz looked pretty much like two of the people on my list. Hawk and I looked at the Identikit sketches and agreed that they were.

"You doing pretty good," Hawk said. "That's six."

"You didn't waste a lot of time when you came through the door."

"Like halt or I'll shoot, that jive?"

"What did you do," I said, "follow Big Nose?"

"Sort of. I spotted him when he come out looking around and I figured he was checking if this was a setup. So I slipped in the hallway there and hid in the shadows back under the stairwell. You know how hard we is to spot in the dark."

"Unless you smile," I said.

"And if we keeps our eyes closed."

We were having breakfast in the hotel. Pastry and cold cuts and butter and cheese buffet style.

"Anyway," Hawk said, "he come slipping back in and

when he open the door I come right in back of him." Hawk drank some coffee.

"Who the one we lost with Kathie?" he said.

"Name's Paul, little guy, very tough. He's a lot heavier article than we been dealing with before. He's a real revolutionary, I think. Of one sort or another."

"Palestinian?"

"I don't think so," I said. "Right wing. Wants to save Africa from the Communists and the Nigras."

"South African? Rhodesian?"

"I don't think so. I mean he may be in that now, but he spoke a language more like Spanish. Maybe Portuguese."

"Angola," Hawk said.

I shrugged. "I don't know. Just said he was anti-communist and prowhite. You probably didn't do much to change his attitude."

Hawk grinned. "He got a big job. I hear there's quite some number of Nigras in Africa. He going to have to do a powerful heap of saving."

"Yeah. He may be dippy, but he's no pancake. He's trouble."

Hawk's face was bright and hard. He grinned again.

"So are we, babe," he said.

"True," I said.

"What's the program now?" Hawk said.

"I don't know. I gotta think."

"Okay, while you thinking, why don't we stroll down to Tivoli and walk around. I heard about Tivoli all my life. I want to see it."

"Yeah," I said. "Me too."

I paid the bill and we went out.

Tivoli was nice. Lots of greenery and not too much plastic. We ate lunch on the terrace of one of the restaurants. There wasn't a great deal for adults to do but watch the kids, and quite frequently the kids' moms, as they went here and there on the pleasant walks among the attractive buildings. It was fun to be there, but it was more a matter of presence, of space allotted to pleasure and thoughtfully done, that made it a pleasure. The lunch was ordinary.

"Ain't Coney Island," Hawk said.

"Ain't the Four Seasons either," I said. I was trying to chew a piece of tough veal and it made me grumpy.

"You thought enough yet?" Hawk said.

I nodded, still working on the veal.

"Should of had fish," Hawk said.

"Hate fish," I said. "Right now we are up a fjord without an oar, as we Danes say. Kathie sure as hell isn't going to go back to her apartment. We've lost her and we've lost Paul." I took out my pocket notebook.

"What I have got is an address in Amsterdam and one in Montreal that I took off her passports. I also have an address in Amsterdam that was the return address on a letter she got, and kept. The addresses are the same."

"Sounds like Amsterdam," Hawk said. He sipped some champagne and watched a young blond woman with very tight shorts and a halter top stroll by. "Too bad, Copenhagen looks good."

"Amsterdam's better," I said. "You'll like it." Hawk shrugged. I dug out some English pounds and gave them to Hawk. "You better get some new clothes. While you do that I'll set us up to Amsterdam. You can probably change the money to kroner at the railroad station. It's right across the street."

"I change it at the hotel, babe. Thought I might leave the shotgun home while I trying on clothes. Three folks got done in with a shotgun yesterday. I just as leave not explain to the Danish fuzz about what we doing."

Hawk left. I paid the bill and headed out the front exit

of Tivoli Gardens. Across the street was the huge red brick Copenhagen railroad station. I went across the street and went in. I had nothing to do there but it was everything a European railroad station ought to be and I wanted to walk around in it. It was high ceilinged and arcane with an enormous barrel-arched central waiting room full of restaurants and shops, baggage rooms, backpacker kids and a babble of foreign tongues. Trains were leaving on various tracks for Paris and Rome, for Munich and Belgrade. And the station was alive with excitement, with coming and going. I loved it. I walked around for nearly an hour by myself, soaking it up. Thinking about Europe in the nineteenth century when it had peaked. The station was thick with life.

Ah Suze, I thought, *you should have been here, you should have seen this*. Then I went back to the hotel and had the hall porter book us a flight to Amsterdam in the morning.

17

The KLM 727 came sweeping in low over Holland at about nine-thirty-five in the morning. I'd been there before and I liked it. It felt familiar and easy as I looked down at the flat green land patterned with canals. We were drinking awful coffee handed out by a KLM stewardess with hairy armpits.

"Don't care for the armpit," Hawk murmured.

"Can't say I do myself," I said.

"You know what it reminds me of?"

"Yes."

Hawk laughed. "Thought you would, babe. You think old Kathie gonna be in Amsterdam?"

"Hell, I don't know. It was the best I could do. Better bet than Montreal. It's closer and I got the same address from two different sources. Or she could have stayed in Denmark or gone to Pakistan. All we can do is look."

"You the boss. You keep paying me, I keep looking. Where we staying?"

"The Marriott, it's up near the Rijksmuseum. If it's slow I'll take you over and show you the Rembrandts."

"Hot dawg," Hawk said.

The seat belt sign went on, the plane settled another notch down and ten minutes later we were on the ground. Schiphol Airport was shiny and glassy and new like the airport in Copenhagen. We got a bus into the Amsterdam railroad station, which wasn't bad but didn't match up to Copenhagen, and a cab from the station to the Marriott Hotel.

The Marriott was part of the American chain, a big new hotel, modern and color-coordinated and filled with the continental charm of a Mobil Station.

Hawk and I shared a room on the eighth floor. No point to concealing our relationship. If we found Kathie or Paul, they'd seen Hawk and would be looking over their shoulder for him again.

After we unpacked we strolled out to find the address on Kathie's passport.

Much of Amsterdam was built in the seventeenth century, and the houses along the canals looked like a Vermeer painting. The streets that separated the houses from the canals were cobbled and there were trees. We followed Leidsestraat toward the Dam Square, crossing the concentric canals as we went: Prinsengracht, Keisersgracht, Heerengracht. The water was dirty green, but it didn't seem to matter much. What cars there were were small and unobtrusive. There were bicycles and a lot of walkers. Boats, often glass-topped tour boats, cruised by on the canals. A lot of the walkers were kids with long hair and jeans and backpacks who gave no hint of nationality and very little of gender. Back when people used to speak that way, Amsterdam was said to be the hippie capital of Europe.

Hawk was watching everything. Walking soundlessly, apparently self-absorbed, as if listening to some inward music. I noticed people gave way to him as he walked, instinctively, without thought.

The Leidsestraat was shopping district. The shops were good-looking and the clothes contemporary. There was

Delftware and imitation Delftware in some quantity. There were cheese shops, and bookstores and restaurants, and a couple of wonderful-looking delicatessens with whole hams and roast geese and baskets of currants in the windows. On the square near the Mint Tower there was a herring stand.

"Try that, Hawk," I said. "You're into fish."

"Raw?"

"Yeah. Last time I was here people raved about them."

"Why don't you try one then?"

"I hate fish."

Hawk bought a raw herring from the stand. The woman at the stand cut it up, sprinkled it with raw onions and handed it to him. Hawk tried a bite.

He smiled. "Not bad," he said. "Ain't chitlins, but it ain't bad."

"Hawk," I said, "I bet you don't know what a goddamned chitlin is."

"Ah spec dat's right, bawse. I was raised on moon pies and Kool-Aid, mostly. It's called ghetto soul."

Hawk ate the rest of the herring. We bore left past the herring stand and turned down the Kalverstraat. It was a pedestrian street, no cars, devoted to shops.

"It's like Harvard Square," Hawk said.

"Yeah, a lot of stores that sell Levi's and Frye boots and peasant blouses. What the hell you doing in Harvard Square?"

"Used to shack up with a Harvard lady," Hawk said. "Very smart."

"Student?"

"No, man, I'm no chicken tapper. She was a professor. Told me I had a elemental power that turned her on. Haw."

"How'd you get along with her seeing-eye dog?"

"Shit, man. She could see. She thought I was gorgeous.

Called me her savage, man. Said Adam musta looked like me."

"Jesus, Hawk, I'm going to puke on your shoe in a minute."

"Yeah, I know. It was awful. We didn't last long. She too weird for me. Surely could screw though. Strong pelvis, you know, man, strong."

"Yeah," I said, "me too. I think this is the place."

We were at an open-front bookstore. There were books and periodicals in racks and on tables out front and rows of them inside. Many of the books were in English. A sign on the wall said THREE HOT SEX SHOWS EVERY HOUR, and an arrow pointed toward the back of the store. In back was another sign that said the same thing with an arrow pointing downstairs.

"What kind of books they sell here?" Hawk said.

There were all kinds, books by Faulkner and Thomas Mann, books in English and books in French, books in Dutch. There was Shakespeare and Gore Vidal and a collection of bondage magazines with nude women on the cover so encumbered in chains, ropes, gags and leather restraints that it was hard to see them. You could buy *Hustler, Time, Paris Match, Punch,* and *Gay Love.* It was one of the things about Amsterdam that I never got over. At home you found a place that sold bondage porn sequestered in the Combat Zone and specializing. Here the bookstore with the THREE HOT SEX SHOWS EVERY HOUR was between a jewelry store and a bake shop. And it also sold the work of Saul Bellow and Jorge Luis Borges.

Hawk said, "You figure Kathie lives here, we could look on a shelf under K."

"Maybe upstairs," I said. "This is the address."

"Yeah," Hawk said. "There's a door."

It was just to the right of the bookstore, half obscured by the awning.

"Think she in there?"

"I know how we find out."

Hawk grinned. "Yeah. We watch. You want to take the first shift while I make sure she not down there among the hot sex films?"

"I didn't figure you for a looker, Hawk. I figured you for a doer."

"Maybe pick up a trick or two. Man's never too old to learn a little. Nobody's perfect."

"Yeah."

"We gonna go round the clock on this, babe?"

"No. Just daytime."

"That's good. Twelve on, twelve off ain't no fish fry."

"This time out it'll be harder. If she's in there she knows us both, and she's going to be very edgy."

"Also," Hawk said, "we camp out here long enough a Dutch cop going to come along and ask us what we doing."

"If they're any good."

"Yeah."

"We'll circulate," I said. "I'll stay up there by the dress shop for a half hour, then I'll stroll down to the place that sells broodjes and you stroll up to the dress shop. And we'll rotate that way every half hour or so."

"Yeah, okay," Hawk said, "let's make the circulation irregular. Each time we switch we'll decide how long before we switch again. Break up the rhythm."

"Yes. We'll do that. Unless there's a back way she'll have to pass one of us if she leaves."

"Why don't you anchor here for a while, babe, and I'll go around and see if I find any back way. I'll check in the

store and I'll go around the block and see what I can
find.''

I nodded. "If she comes out and I go after her I'll meet
you back at the hotel."

Hawk said, "Yowzah" and went into the bookstore. He
went to the back and down the stairs. Five minutes later he
was back up the stairs and out of the bookstore, his face
glistening with humor.

"Get any pointers?" I said.

"Oh yeah, soon's I make a move on a pony, I gonna
know just what to do."

"These Europeans are so sophisticated."

18

Hawk found no back entrance. We walked up and down a short stretch of the Kalverstraat all the rest of the day, staying close to the wall under Kathie's windows, if they were Kathie's windows, so she wouldn't spot us, if she were looking out, if she were up there.

The dress shop was featuring that season a fatigue green number that looked like a shelter half, long and formless, belted at the waist. It didn't even look good on the window dummy. The broodje shop was featuring roast beef on a soft roll, topped with a fried egg. Broodje seemed to mean sandwich. There were about thirty-five different kinds of broodjes listed behind the counter, but the roast beef with the fried egg was the hot seller.

The street was crowded all afternoon. There seemed to be a lot of tourists, Japanese and Germans with cameras, in groups. There was a fair number of Dutch sailors. More people seemed to smoke in Holland than they did at home. And there were far fewer big men. Sandals and clogs seemed more prevalent, especially for men, and occasionally a Dutch cop would stroll by in his gray-blue uniform with white trim. Nobody bothered me and nobody bothered Hawk.

At eight o'clock I said to Hawk, "It is time to go eat before I break into tears."

"I can dig that," Hawk said.

"There's a place just off to the side here called The Little Nun. I ate there last time I was here."

"What you doing here before, man?"

"Pleasure trip. Came with a lady."

"Suze?"

"Yeah."

The Little Nun was everything I remembered. Polished stone floor, whitewashed walls, low-beamed ceiling, some stained glass in the windows, flowers and very fine food. For dessert they brought out a great crock of red currants, cherries, strawberries, raspberries and blackberries that had been marinated in cassis. Everyone spoke English. In fact everyone in Holland spoke English as far as I could tell, and spoke it with very little accent.

We went to bed in the Marriott feeling good about supper but bad about tomorrow. I had the feeling that a lot of aimless walking was in store for us tomorrow.

It was. We walked up and down the Kalverstraat all day. I looked in every store window along the way until I knew the price of all the merchandise. I ate five broodjes during the day, three out of hunger and two out of boredom. The high point of the day was two trips to the public urinal near the Dutch Tourist Bureau on Rokin.

At night we had an Indonesian rijsttafel at the Bali Restaurant on Leidsestraat. There were about twenty-five different courses of meat, vegetables and rice. We drank Amstel beer with the meal. Hawk too. Champagne didn't go with a rijsttafel. Hawk drank some Amstel and said to me, "Spenser, how long we gonna walk up and down past the hot sex shows?"

"I don't know," I said. "We only been at it two days."

"Yeah, man, but we don't even know she's in there. I

mean we may be walking up and down in front of some old Dutch granny.''

"But no one has come out of that place or gone in it in two days. Isn't that a little strange?''

"Maybe nobody lives there.''

I ate some beef with peanuts. "We'll give it another day, then we'll go in and see, okay?''

Hawk nodded. "I like going in and seeing,'' he said, "a lot better than hanging around and watching.''

"I knew you were a doer,'' I said.

"I am that,'' he said. "And I want to do something pretty quick.''

We walked back to the Marriott through night life and music along the Leidsestraat. The lobby was nearly empty. There were two kids from a South American soccer team half asleep in chairs. A bellhop leaned on the counter talking to the desk clerk. Faint music from the in-house night spot drifted down toward the elevators. We rode to the eighth floor in silence. At our room the DO NOT DISTURB sign was on the door. I looked at Hawk, he shook his head. The sign had not been there this morning. I put my ear hard against the door. I could hear the bedsprings creak, and what sounded like heavy breathing. I motioned Hawk to the door. He listened.

We had a room near the corner, and I gestured Hawk around the corner.

"Sound like one of them hot sex shows,'' Hawk said. "You think somebody shacking up in our room?''

"That's crazy,'' I said.

"Maybe a maid or something, see we're out all day, figures she'll slip in with her old man and make it while we out.''

"If you can think of it somebody will do it,'' I said. "But I don't believe it.''

"We could stand around out here awhile and see if they come out. If there's somebody in there putting the boots to his old lady, they can't stay all night."

"I been standing around in hotel corridors and on street corners since I been in Europe. I'm getting sick of it."

"Let's do it," Hawk said. He pulled the shotgun out from under his coat.

I took out the room key and we went around the corner. There was no one in the hall.

Hawk sprawled on the floor in front of the door. I slipped the key in the door. Hawk leveled the shotgun on his propped elbows and nodded. I turned the key from one side of the door out of the line of fire and swung the door open. I had my gun out.

Hawk said, "Jesus Christ," and gestured with his head.

I slid around the door, staying flat against the wall. There were two dead men on the floor and Kathie on the bed. She wasn't dead. She was tied. I kicked open the door to the bathroom. No one there. Hawk was in behind me. He closed the room door with his left hand. The right kept the shotgun half erect in front of him. I came out of the bathroom.

"Nothing," I said, and slid my gun back in its holster.

Hawk squatted beside the two men on the floor. "They dead," he said.

I nodded. Kathie lay on the bed, her hands tied behind her, her feet bound. Her mouth was taped, and a rope around her waist fastened her to the bed.

Hawk looked down at her and said, "That what we heard. Nobody screwing, old Kathie here trying to get loose."

Kathie made a thick muffled sound of outrage and twisted against the ropes.

"What killed the stiffs on the floor?" I said.

"Somebody shot each of them behind the left ear with a small bullet."

"Twenty-two?"

"Could be. Been a while, they pretty cold."

There was an envelope stuck to Kathie's right thigh with some of the same adhesive tape that closed her mouth. I picked it up.

"Maybe we won her in a raffle," I said.

"I bet that ain't it," Hawk said. He was still holding the shotgun, but now negligently, hanging loosely at his side.

I opened the note. Kathie squirmed on the bed and made her muffled noise some more. Hawk read over my shoulder. The note said:

> We have much to do and you are in the way. Had we the time we would kill you. But you are obviously hard to kill, as is the *Schwartze*. Thus we have delivered to you what you seek. The two dead men are the last of those you sought. I shall probably be sorry that I let the woman live, but I am more sentimental than I should be. We have cared for each other and I cannot kill her.
>
> You have no reason now to bother us further. If you persist despite that we shall turn our full attention to your deaths.
>
> Paul.

"Sonovabitch," I said.

"*Schwartze?*" Hawk said.

"That's German for spade, I think."

"I know what it mean," Hawk said. "These two look like your sketches?"

"We'll look," I said. I got the Identikit drawings out of

the top bureau drawer. With his foot Hawk turned both bodies over on their backs. I looked at the pictures and at the phony-looking dead faces staring up at me. "I'd say so." I handed the drawings to Hawk.

He nodded. "Look about right," he said.

I pointed my chin at Kathie. "And that makes number nine."

"What you going to do?"

"We could untie her."

"You think we safe?"

"There's two of us," I said.

"She awful mean and mad-looking," Hawk said.

He was right. Kathie's eyes were wide and angry. Since we had entered the room she had not stopped twisting against the ropes, squirming to get free. She grunted furiously at us.

"Actually, you know, we better pat her down. It could be a very elaborate fake. We untie her and she jumps up and shoots us."

Hawk laughed. "You are a suspicious mamma." He put the shotgun down on the night table. "But I'll check her."

I looked out the window at the street eight floors below. Nothing looked different than it should. Across the street in the light of street lamps the canal flowed past. A tour boat taking a candlelight cruise glimmered by. They served wine and cheese on the candlelight cruises. If I were with Suze we could drift through the ancient graceful city and drink the wine and eat the cheese and have a nice time. But Suze wasn't here. Hawk would probably go with me, but I didn't think he'd care for the hand-holding.

I looked back at Hawk. He was methodically patting Kathie for a hidden weapon. As he did so she began to twist and squirm, and a high locust sort of noise forced out around the tape. As he touched her thighs she arched her back and, straining against the ropes, thrust her pelvis forward. Her face was very red and her breath came in snorts through her nose.

Hawk looked at me. "She ain't armed," he said.

I reached down and carefully peeled the tape from her mouth. She breathed in gasps through her open mouth, reddened from the friction of the tape.

"Shall you," she gasped, "shall you rape me? Shall he?" She looked at Hawk. The locust hum in her voice had softened to a kind of hiss. A little saliva bubbled at the left corner of her mouth. Her body continued to arch against the ropes.

"I'm not sure it would be rape," I said.

"Shall you both take me, gag me again. Take me while I'm helpless, voiceless, bound and writhing on the bed?"

Her mouth was open now and her tongue ran and fretted over her lower lip.

"I can't move," she gasped. "I'm bound and helpless, shall you tear my clothing, use me, degrade me, drive me mad?"

Hawk said, "Naw."

I said, "Maybe later."

Hawk pulled a jackknife from his right hip pocket and cut her free. He had to roll her over to cut the rope on her hands, and when he did he gave her a slap on the backside, light and friendly, like one ballplayer to another. She sat up abruptly.

"Nigger," she said. "Never touch me, nigger."

Hawk looked at me, his face bright. "Nigger?" he said.

"That's English for spade, I think."

"I know what it mean," Hawk said.

"What happened to take me, ravage me?" I said.

"I'll kill you both," she said, "as soon as I can."

"That gonna be awhile, hon," Hawk said. "Beside you gonna have to get in line."

She was sitting up now on the edge of the bed. Her white linen dress was badly wrinkled from her struggle against the ropes. "I want to go to the bathroom," she said.

"Go ahead," I said. "Take your time."

She walked stiffly to the bathroom and closed the door. We heard the bolt slide and then the water begin to run in the sink. Hawk walked over to one of the red vinyl armchairs, stepped carefully over the two dead men on the floor.

"What we going to do with the corpus delicti here?" Hawk said.

"Oh," I said. "You don't know either?"

19

While Kathie was still in the bathroom, Hawk and I took one body each and slipped them under the twin beds.

In the bathroom, the faucet still ran in the sink, masking any other sound. "What you suppose she doing?" Hawk said.

"Nothing probably. She's probably trying to think what to do when she comes out."

"Maybe she perfuming up in case we want to rape her."

"Still waters run deep," I said. "Her idea of a good time is probably to be beaten by Benito Mussolini with a copy of *Mein Kampf*."

"Or to be raped by you and me," Hawk said.

"Especially you, big fella. I know what they say about you black folk."

"And quick," Hawk said, "we very quick and rhythmical."

"That's what I heard," I said.

I got a can of Spot-lifter off the top closet shelf and sprayed the blood stains on the rug.

"That stuff work?"

"Works on my suits," I said. "When it dries I just brush it away."

"You make a fine wife someday, babe. You cook good too."

"Yeah, but I've always wanted a career of my own."

Kathie shut off the running water and came out of the bathroom. She'd combed her hair and smoothed out her dress as much as possible.

I was on my hands and knees working on the blood stains. "Sit down," I said. "You want something to eat? Drink? Both?"

"I am hungry," she said.

"Hawk, get her something from room service."

"They got a late night special here," Hawk said. "House pâté, cheese, bread and a carafe of wine. Want that?"

Kathie nodded. "That sounds pretty good," I said to Hawk. "Why don't we all have some."

"That how it is eating that Indonesian food," Hawk said. "An hour later you hungry again."

Kathie sat in one of the straight chairs near the window, her hands in her lap, her knees together. Her head lowered looking at the crossed thumbs of her clasped hands. Hawk called and ordered. I brushed away the dried Spot-lifter and applied some cold water to what was left of the blood stain.

The room service waiter appeared with the late night special and Hawk took the table from him at the door. Hawk set the circular table into the room with the pâté and cheese, French bread and red wine.

"Go ahead, kid," Hawk said to Kathie. "Sit down, we gonna eat."

Kathie came to the table and sat down without a word. Hawk poured her some wine. She drank a little and her hand shook enough so that some spilled on her chin. She wiped it with a napkin. Hawk cut a wedge of pâté and broke a piece of bread and said to me, "What we gonna do with Kathie?"

"Don't know," I said. I drank some wine. It had a rich mouth-filling taste. Maybe the people who didn't chill it knew what they were about.

"How about what we doing here. I mean, we gonna do what the note said? We done what you was hired for?"

"Don't know," I said. "This pâté is terrific."

"Yeah," Hawk said. "These little nuts pistachios?"

"Yeah," I said. "You want to go home?"

"Me, man? I got nothing to go home to. It's you getting moony about Susan and all."

"Yeah."

"Besides," Hawk said, "I don't like that Paul."

"Yeah."

"I don't like how he was gonna kill us, and I don't like him saying he will if we keep after him, and I don't like much how he dump his girlfriend on us when we get close."

"No. I don't like that much either. I don't like walking away from him."

"Besides," Hawk's face widened into a brilliant humorless smile, "he call me *Schwartze*."

"Racist bastard," I said.

"Whyn't we tell him we ain't taking the deal."

Kathie ate and drank in silence.

"You know where he is, Kathie?"

She shook her head. There seemed no more venom in her.

Hawk said, "Sure you do. You must have some place where you people make contact if you get in trouble."

She shook her head. Tears had begun to run down her cheeks.

Hawk took a sip of wine, put down the glass and

slapped her across the face. Her head rocked back and then she seemed to collapse in on herself, shrinking down into the chair. The tears came in sobs then, shaking her body as she bent over. She put both hands over her ears and squeezed her face between her forearms and cried. Hawk sipped some more wine and looked at her with mild interest.

"She do take on," he said.

"She's scared," I said. "Everybody gets scared. She's alone with two guys she's tried to kill and the man she loves has ditched her. She's alone. That's hard."

"It gonna get a lot harder if she don't tell us what I want her to," Hawk said.

"Beating up on a lady isn't your style, Hawk."

"Women's lib, babe. She got the same rights to have me bust her up that a man have."

"I don't like it."

"Take a walk then. When you come back, we'll know what we want to know."

I stood up. I knew we were playing good-cop bad-cop, but did Hawk?

"Oh my God," Kathie said. "Don't."

Hawk stood up too. He took off the jacket, slipped out of the shotgun shoulder rig and peeled off his shirt. Hawk had always had a lot of muscle tone. His upper body was taut and graceful. The muscles in his chest and arms swelled slightly as he made a slight loosening gesture with his shoulders. I started for the door.

"Oh God, don't leave me with him." Kathie slid out of the chair onto the floor and crawled after me. "Don't let him. Don't let him debase me. Please don't."

Hawk stepped between her and me. She grasped one of his legs. "Don't, don't, don't." The saliva was bubbling again at the corner of her mouth. She was gasping for breath. Her nose ran.

I said to Hawk, "I don't want to know this bad."

"Your biggest problem, man, you a candy ass."

I shrugged. "I still don't want to know this bad." I reached down and took Kathie's arm. "Get up," I said. "And sit in the chair. We aren't going to do anything bad to you." I put her in the chair. Then I went in the bathroom and got a facecloth and soaked it in cold water and wrung it out and brought it in and washed her face with it.

Hawk looked like he was going to puke. I gave her a glass of wine. "Drink some," I said. "And get it back together. Take your time. We got lots of time. When you're ready, we'll talk a little. Okay?"

Kathie nodded.

Hawk said, "You remember she blew up some guy's wife and kids? You remember she trying to set you up in the London Zoo? You remember she gonna stand around while her boyfriend wasted you in Copenhagen? You remember what she is?"

"I'm not worrying about what she is," I said. "I'm worrying about what I am."

"Gonna get you killed someday, babe."

"We'll do it my way, Hawk."

"You paying the money, babe, you can pick the music." He put his shirt back on.

We ate the rest of the late night special in silence.

"Okay, Kathie. Is that your name?"

"It is one of them."

"Well, I'm used to thinking of you as Kathie so I'll stick with it."

She nodded. Her eyes were red but dry. She slumped as she sat.

"Tell me about you and your group, Kathie."

"I should tell you nothing."

"Why? Who do you owe? Who is there to be loyal to?"
She looked at her lap.

"Tell me about you and your group."

"It is Paul's group."

"What is it for?"

"It is for keeping Africa white."

Hawk snorted.

"Keeping," I said.

"Keeping the control in white hands. Keeping the blacks from destroying what white civilization had made of Africa." She wouldn't look at Hawk.

"And how was blowing up some people in a London restaurant going to do that?"

"The British were wrong on Rhodesia and wrong on South Africa. It was punishment."

Hawk had stood and gone to the window. He was whistling "Saint James Infirmary Blues" through his teeth as he stood looking down into the street.

"What were you doing in England?"

"Organizing the English unit. Paul sent me."

"Any connection with IRA?"

"No."

"Try?"

"Yes."

"They're only concerned with their own hatreds," I said. "Are there many more left in England of your unit?"

"No. You . . . you overcame us all."

"Gonna overcome all the rest of you too," Hawk said from the window.

Kathie looked blank.

"What's shaking in Copenhagen?"

"I don't understand."

"Why did you go to Denmark when you left London?"

"Paul was there."

"What was he doing there?"

"He lives there sometimes. He lives many places and that's one of them."

"The apartment on Vester Søgade?"

"Yes."

"And when Hawk busted that up you and he came here."

"Yes."

"The address on the Kalverstraat?"

"Yes."

"And you spotted us watching?"

"Paul did. He is very careful."

I looked at Hawk. Hawk said, "He pretty good too. I never saw him."

"And?"

"And he called me on the telephone and made me stay inside. Then he watched you while you watched me. When you left for the night he came in."

"When?"

"Last night."

"And you moved out of that place?"

"Yes, to Paul's apartment."

"And today while we were staking out the empty place on the Kalverstraat, Paul brought you and the two stiffs here."

"Yes, Milo and Antone. They thought we were coming to ambush you. I did too."

"And when you got in here Paul burned Milo and Antone?"

"Excuse me?"

"Paul killed the two men."

"Paul and a man named Zachary. Paul said it was time for a sacrifice. Then he bound me and gagged me and left me for you. He said he was sorry."

"Where's the apartment?"

"It doesn't matter. They won't be there."

"Tell me anyway."

"It's on the Prinsengracht." She told us the number. I looked at Hawk.

He nodded, slipped into the shotgun rig, put on his jacket and went out. Hawk needed a shotgun less than most.

"What are Paul's plans now?"

"I don't know."

"You must know something. Until last night you were his darling."

Her eyes filled.

"And now you aren't. You should start getting used to that."

She nodded.

"So being as you were his darling up till today, didn't he tell you anything about his plans?"

"He told no one. When he was ready we were told what to do, but not before."

"So you didn't know what was coming down tomorrow?"

"I don't understand."

"You didn't even know what was going to be done tomorrow."

"That is right."

"And you don't think he's at the place on Prinsengracht?"

"No. No one will be there when the black man gets there."

"His name is Hawk," I said.

She nodded.

"If the police penetrated your organization, or if they raided the apartment on Prinsengracht, where would the survivors meet?"

"We have a calling system. Each person has two people to call."

"Who were you supposed to call?"

"Milo and Antone."

"Balls."

"I cannot help you."

"Maybe you can't," I said. And maybe she couldn't. Maybe I'd used her up.

20

Hawk was back in less than an hour. When he came in he shook his head.

"Gone?" I said.

"Uh huh."

"Clues?"

Hawk said, "Clues?"

"You know," I said, "like an airplane schedule with a flight to Beirut underlined. A hotel confirmation slip from the Paris Hilton. Some tourist brochures from Orange County, California. A tinkling piano in the next apartment. Clues."

"No clues, man."

"Anyone see them leave?"

"Nope."

"So the only thing we know for sure is he isn't in his place on Prinsengracht, and he isn't here in this room."

"He wasn't when I looked. She tell you anything?"

"Everything she knows."

"Maybe you believe that, babe. I don't."

"We've been trying. You want some more wine? I ordered some while you were gone."

"Yeah."

I poured some for Hawk and some for Kathie. "Okay, kid," I said to Kathie. "He's gone and all we've got is you. Where might he be?"

"He could be anywhere," she said. Her face was a little flushed. She'd had a lot of wine. "He can go anywhere in the world."

"Phony passport?"

"Yes. I don't know how many. Many."

Hawk had taken off his coat and hung the shotgun rig from the corner of a chair. He was leaning far back with his Frye boots crossed on the bureau and the glass of red wine balanced on his chest. His eyes almost closed.

"Where would the places be that he wouldn't go?"

"I don't understand."

"I going too fast for you, sugar? Watch my lips close. Where would he not go?"

Kathie drank some wine. She looked at Hawk the way sparrows are supposed to look at tree snakes. It was a look of fearful fascination.

"I don't know."

"She don't know," Hawk said to me. "You do take up with some winners, babe."

"What the hell are you going to do, Hawk, keep eliminating the places he wouldn't go until there's only one left?"

"You got a better idea, babe?"

"No. Where would he be least likely to go, Kathie?"

"I cannot say."

"Think a little. Would he go to Russia?"

"Oh no."

"Red China?"

"No, no. No Communist country."

Hawk made a gesture of triumph with his open palms turned up. "See, babe, eliminate half the world just like that."

"Swell," I said. "This sounds like an old Abbott and Costello routine."

Hawk said, "You know a better game?"

Kathie said, "Have they had the Olympics yet?"

Hawk and I looked at her. "The Olympic games?"

"Yes."

"They're on now."

"Last year he sent away for tickets to the Olympic games. Where are they being held?"

Hawk and I said, "In Montreal," at the same time.

Kathie drank some wine and made a small giggle and said, "Well, that's probably where he went, then."

I said, "Why in hell didn't you tell us?"

"I didn't think of it. I don't know about sports. I didn't even know when they were being held or where. I just know Paul had tickets for them."

Hawk said, "It's pretty much on the way home anyway, man."

"There's a restaurant in Montreal called Bacco's that you're going to like," I said.

"What we do with fancy pants here?" Hawk said.

"Please don't be dirty."

The white linen dress was very simple, square-necked and straight-lined. She had a thick silver chain around her neck and white sling high-heeled shoes with no stockings. Her wrists and ankles were red and marked from the ropes. Her mouth was red and her eyes were puffy and red. Her hair was matted and tangled from her long struggle on the bed. "I don't know," I said, "she's all we have."

"I'll go with you," she said. Her voice was small when she said it. Quite different from the one she'd used when she said she'd kill us when she could. Didn't mean she'd changed her mind. But it didn't mean she hadn't. I figured between us we could keep her from killing us.

"She change sides awful fast," Hawk said.

"They got changed on her," I said. "We'll take her. She may be helpful."

"She may stick something in us when we ain't looking too."

"One of us will always look," I said. "She knows this Zachary. We don't. If he's in on this he might be there. Maybe others. She's the only thing connected to Paul we have. We'll keep her."

Hawk shrugged and drank some wine.

"In the morning we'll check out and get the first flight we can to Montreal."

"What about the two stiffs?"

"We'll ditch them in the morning."

"Hope they don't start to stink before then."

"We can't ditch them before that. The cops will be all over the place. We'll never get out of here. What time is it?"

"It's three-thirty."

"About nine-thirty in Boston. Too late to call Jason Carroll. I only got his office number anyway."

"Who Jason Carroll?"

"Dixon's lawyer. He's sort of in charge of this thing. I'll feel better when I've talked with Dixon about our plans."

"Maybe your wallet feel better too."

"No, I think this one will be on me. But Dixon's got a right to know what's going on."

"And I got a right to sleep. Who she sleep with?"

"I'll put a mattress off the floor and she can sleep on the box spring."

"She look disappointed. I think she had another plan."

Kathie said, "May I take a bath?"

I said, "Sure."

I dragged the mattress off the bed closest to the door, and

stretched it out across the doorway. Kathie went into the bathroom and closed the door. The lock snicked into place. I could hear the water running in the tub.

Hawk stripped to his shorts and got into bed. He took the shotgun under the covers with him. I lay down on the mattress with my pants still on. I put my gun under the pillow. It made a lump, but not as big a lump as it would make in my body if Kathie got it in the night. The lights were out and just a thin line of light came under the bathroom door. As I lay in the dark I began to smell, only vaguely so far, a smell I'd smelled before. It was the smell of bodies that had been dead too long. It would have been a lot worse without air conditioning. It wouldn't get better before morning.

Tired as I was, I didn't sleep until Kathie came out of the bathroom and stepped across me and went to bed on the box spring of the near bed.

21

In the morning after we checked out, Hawk stole a laundry hamper from a utility closet whose lock I picked. We put the two bodies in the hamper, covered them with dirty linen, put the hamper in an empty elevator and sent the elevator to the top floor. We did all this while keeping a close eye on Kathie, who didn't show any sign of wanting to bolt. Or kill us. She seemed to want to stay with us as badly as we wanted her. Or I wanted her. I think Hawk would have dropped her in a canal if he'd been on his own.

We got a bus from the KLM terminal in Museumplein and caught a KLM flight from Schiphol to London at nine-fifty-five, connecting with an Air Canada flight to Montreal at noon. At one-fifteen London time I was sitting on the outside seat with Kathie next to me and Hawk on the window, drinking a Labatt 50 ale and waiting for the meal to be served. Six hours later, early afternoon Montreal time, we set down in Canada, changed money, collected luggage, and by three o'clock we were standing in line at the Olympic housing office in Place Ville Marie waiting to get lodging. By four-fifteen we had gotten to the man at the desk, and by quarter of six we were in a rented Ford heading out Boulevard St. Laurent for an address near Boulevard Henri Bourassa. I felt like I had gone fifteen rounds with Dino the Boxing Rhinoceros. Even Hawk looked a little tired, and Kathie seemed to be asleep in the back seat of the car.

The address was one half of a duplex on a side street a block from Henri Bourassa Boulevard. The name was Boucher. The husband spoke English, the wife and daughter only French. They were going to their summer home on a lake and were picking up two weeks' worth of rent leasing their home to Olympic visitors. I gave them the voucher from the Olympic housing office. They smiled and showed us where things were. The wife spoke to Kathie in French, showing her the laundry and where the cookware was kept. Kathie looked blank. Hawk answered her in very polite French.

When they had gone and left us the key I said to Hawk, "Where'd you come up with the French?"

"I done some time in the Foreign Legion, babe, when things was sorta mean in Boston. You dig?"

"Hawk, you amaze me. Vietnam?"

"Yeah, and Algeria, all of that."

"Beau Geste," I said.

"The lady she think Kathie your wife," Hawk said. He smiled very wide. "I told her she your daughter and she don't know much about cooking and things."

"I told the man we brought you along to stand outside in a jockey suit and hold horses."

"Ah'm powerful good at sittin' on a bale of cotton and singin' 'Old Black Joe' too, bawse."

Kathie sat at the counter in the small kitchen and watched us without understanding.

The house was small and lovingly done. The kitchen was pine-paneled and the cabinets were new. The adjoining dining room had an antique table and on the wall a pair of antlers, obviously home-shot. The living room had little furniture and a worn rug. Everything was clean and careful. In one corner was an old television with the screen outlined in white, giving the illusion of greater screen size. There were three small bedrooms upstairs, and a bath. One of the bedrooms was obviously a room for boys, with twin beds, two bureaus and a host of wildlife pictures and stuffed animals. The bathroom was pink.

It was a house that its owners loved. It made me ill at ease to be here with Hawk and Kathie. We had no business in a house like this.

Hawk went out and bought some beer and wine and cheese and French bread, and we ate and drank in near silence. After supper Kathie went up to one of the small bedrooms, filled with dolls and dust ruffles, and went to bed, with her clothes on. She still wore the white linen dress. It was getting pretty wrinkled but there wasn't a change of clothes. Hawk and I watched some of the Olympic action on CBC. We were on the wrong side of the mountain to get U.S. stations and thus most of the coverage focused on Canadians, not many of whom were in medal contention.

We finished up the beer and wine and went to bed before eleven o'clock, exhausted from traveling and silent and out of place in the quiet suburb among artifacts of family.

I slept in the boys' room, Hawk in the master bedroom. There were early bird sounds but the room was still dark when I woke up and saw Kathie standing at the foot of the bed. The door was closed behind her. She turned the light on. Her breath in the silence was short and heavy. She wore no clothes. She was the kind of woman who should take her clothes off when she can. She looked best without them; the proportions were better than they looked dressed. She did not seem to be carrying a concealed weapon. I was naked and on top of the covers in the warm summer. It embarrassed me. I slid under the sheet until I was covered from the waist down and rolled on to my back.

I said, "Hard to sleep these hot nights, isn't it?"

She walked across the room and dropped to her knees beside the bed and settled back with her buttocks resting on her heels.

"Maybe a little warm milk," I said.

She took my left hand where it was resting on my chest and pulled it over to her and held it between her breasts.

"Sometimes counting sheep helps," I said. My voice was getting a little hoarse.

Her breath was very short, as if she'd been sprinting, and the place between her breasts was damp with sweat. She said, "Do with me what you will."

"Wasn't that the title of a book?" I said.

"I'll do anything," she said. "You may have me. I'll be your slave. Anything." She bent over, keeping my hand between her breasts and began to kiss me on the chest. Her hair smelled strongly of shampoo and her body of soap. She must have bathed before she came in.

"I'm not into slaves, Kath," I said.

Her kisses were moving down over my stomach. I felt like a pubescent billy goat.

"Kathie," I said. "I barely know you. I mean I thought we were just friends."

She kept kissing. I sat up in bed and pulled my hand away from her sternum. She slid onto the bed as I made room, her whole body insinuated against me, her left hand running along my back. "Strong," she gasped. "Strong, so strong. Press me down, force me."

I took hold of both her hands at the wrists and held them down in front of her. She twisted over and flopped on her back, her legs apart. Her mouth half open, making small creature sounds in her throat. The bedroom door opened and Hawk stood in it in his shorts, crouched slightly, bent for trouble. His face relaxed and broadened into pleasure as he watched.

"Goddamn," he said.

"It's okay, Hawk," I said. "No trouble." My voice was very hoarse.

"I guess not," he said. He closed the door and I could hear his thick velvet laugh in the hall. He said through the closed door, "Hey, Spenser. You want me to stay out here and hum 'Boots and Saddles' sort of soft while you're, ah, subduing the suspect?"

I let that pass. Kathie seemed uninterrupted.

"Him too," she gasped. "Both at once if you wish." She was almost boneless, sprawled on the bed, arms and legs flung out, her body wet with sweat.

"Kathie, you gotta find some other way to relate with people. Killing and screwing have their place but there are other alternatives." I was croaking now. I cleared my throat loudly. My body felt like there was too much blood in it. I was nearly ready to paw the ground and whinny.

"Please," she said, her voice now barely audible, "please."

"No offense, honey, but no."

"Please," she was hissing now. Her body writhed on the bed. She arched her pelvis up, as she had when Hawk searched her in Amsterdam. "Please." I still held her hands.

The more I held her and denied her the more she seemed to respond. It was a form of abuse and it excited her. Embarrassing or not, I had to get up. I slid out from under the sheet and slipped off the bed, rolling over her legs as I did. She used the space I'd left to spread out wider in a position of enlarged vulnerability. One of the animal behaviorists would say she was in extreme submission. I was in extreme randiness. I took my Levis off the chair and put them on. I was careful zipping them up. With them on I felt better.

Kathie was alone now, I think she wasn't even aware of me. Her breath came in thin hisses as it squeezed out between her teeth. She writhed and arched on the bed, the sheets a wet tangle beneath her. I didn't know what to do. I felt like sucking my thumb but Hawk might come in and catch me. I wished Susan were here. I wished I weren't. I sat on the other bed in the room, both feet on the floor, ready to jump if she came for me, and watched her.

The window got gray and then pink. The bird sounds increased, some trucks drove by somewhere outside, not many, and not often. The sun was up. In the other half of the duplex, water ran. Kathie stopped wrenching herself around. I heard Hawk get up next door and the shower start. Kathie's breathing was quiet. I got up and went to my suitcase and took out one of my shirts and handed it to her. "Here," I said. "I don't have a robe, but this might do. Later we'll buy you some clothes."

"Why," she said. Her voice was normal now but flat, and very soft.

"Because you need some. You've been wearing that dress for a couple of days now."

"I mean why didn't you take me?"

"I'm sort of spoken for," I said.

"You don't want me."

"Part of me does, I was jumping out of my skin. But it's not my style. It has to do with love. And, ah, your, your approach wasn't quite right."

"You think I'm corrupt."

"I think you're neurotic."

"You fucking pig."

"That approach doesn't do it either," I said. "Though lots of people have used it on me."

She was quiet, but a pink flush smudged across each cheekbone.

The shower stopped and I heard Hawk walk back to the bedroom.

"I guess I'll shower now," I said. "You ought to be out of here and wearing something when I'm through. Then we'll all have a nice breakfast and plan our day."

My shirt reached nearly to Kathie's knees and she ate breakfast in it, silently, perched on a stool at the counter with her knees together. Hawk sat across the counter, splendid in a bell-sleeved white shirt. He was wearing a gold earring in his right ear, and a thin gold chain tight around his neck. The Bouchers had left some eggs and some white bread. I steam-fried the eggs with a small splash of white wine, and served the toast with apple butter.

Hawk ate with pleasure, his movements exact and sure, like a surgeon, or at least as I hoped a surgeon's would be. Kathie ate without appetite but neatly, leaving most of the eggs and half the toast on her plate.

I said, "There's some kind of clothing store down Boulevard St. Laurent. I saw it when we came up last night. Hawk, why don't you take Kathie down there and get her some clothes?"

"Maybe she rather go with you, babe."

Kathie said in a flat voice, softly, "I'd rather go with you, Hawk." It was the first time I could remember her using his name.

"You ain't gonna make a move on me in the car, are you?"

She dropped her head.

"Go ahead," I said. "I'll clean up here and then I'll think a little."

Hawk said, "Don't hurt yourself."

I said, "Kathie, put on some clothes."

She didn't move and she didn't look at me.

Hawk said, "Come on, girl, shake your ass. You heard the man."

Kathie got up and went upstairs.

Hawk and I looked at each other. Hawk said, "You think she might be about to break the color barrier?"

"It's just that myth about your equipment," I said.

"Ain't no myth, man."

I took $100 Canadian out of my wallet and gave it to Hawk. "Here, buy her a hundred worth of clothes. Whatever she wants. Don't let her blow it on fancy lingerie though."

"From what I seen last night she ain't planning to wear none."

"Maybe tonight is your turn," I said.

"Didn't satisfy her, huh?"

"I didn't come across," I said. "I never do on the first date."

"Admire a man with standards, babe, I surely do. Suze be proud of you."

"Yeah."

"That why she so grouchy about you this morning. That why I looking better to her."

"She's a sicko, Hawk."

"Ah ain't planning to screw her psyche, babe."

I shrugged. Kathie came down the stairs in the wrinkled white linen. She went with Hawk without looking at me. When they were gone I washed the dishes, put everything away, and then I called Dixon's man, Jason Carroll, collect.

"I'm in Montreal," I said. "I have accounted for all the

people on Dixon's list, and I suppose I should come home."

"Yes," Carroll said. "Flanders has been sending us reports and clippings. Mr. Dixon is quite satisfied with the first five. If you can verify the last four . . ."

"We'll get to that when I'm back in town. What I want to do now is talk to Dixon."

"About what?"

"I want to keep on for a while. I have the end of something and I want to pull it all the way out of its hole before I quit."

"You have been paid a good deal of money already, Spenser."

"That's why I want to talk with Dixon. You can't authorize it."

"Well, I don't . . ."

"Call him and tell him I want to talk. Then call me back. Don't act executive with me. We both know you are a glorified go-for."

"That's hardly true, Spenser, but we need not argue about that. I'll be in touch with Mr. Dixon, and I'll call you back. What is your number?"

I read him the number off the phone and hung up. Then I sat down in the sparse living room and thought.

If Paul and Zachary were here, and maybe they were, they had tickets for the Olympics. Kathie had no idea which events. But it was pretty likely that they'd show up at the stadium. It was possible they were sport fans, but it was more likely that, sport fans or not, they had a plan to do in something or someone at the Olympics. A lot of African teams were boycotting, but not all. And on their track record they were pretty loose on who they damaged on behalf of the cause. There wasn't much to be gained by going to the Canadian cops. They were already screwing the security down as tight as they could after the horror show in Munich. If we got to them, all they could do was tell us to stay out of the way. And we didn't want to stay out of the way. So we'd do this without the cops.

If Paul wanted to make a gesture, the Olympic stadium was the place. It was the center of media attention. It was the place to look for him. To do that we needed tickets. I was figuring that Dixon could do that.

The phone rang. It was Carroll. "Mr. Dixon will see you," he said.

"Why not a phone call."

"Mr. Dixon doesn't do business on the phone. He'll see you at his home as soon as you can come."

"Okay. It's an hour flight. I'll be there this afternoon sometime. I'll have to check the flight schedule."

"Mr. Dixon will be there. Any time. He never goes out and he rarely sleeps."

"I'll be there sometime today."

I hung up, called the airport, booked a flight for after lunch. Called Susan Silverman and got no answer. Hawk came back with Kathie. They had four or five bags. Hawk had a long package done in brown paper.

"Picked up a new shotgun at a sporting goods store," he said. "After lunch I'll modify it."

Kathie went upstairs with the bags.

I said to Hawk, "I'm flying to Boston this afternoon, be back tomorrow morning."

"Remember me to Suze," he said.

"If I see her."

"What do you mean if. What you going for?"

"I gotta talk to Dixon. He doesn't talk on the phone."

"You got his bread," Hawk said. "I guess you don't have to do what you don't want."

"You and Kathie can lurk around down at the stadium.

If you can find a scalper you might buy tickets and go in. I figure that's where Paul's likely to show."

"What I want with Kathie?"

"Maybe Zachary will show instead of Paul. Maybe somebody else she might know. Besides, I don't like leaving her alone."

"That ain't what you said this morning."

"You know what I mean."

Hawk grinned. "What you want with Dixon?"

"I need his clout. I need tickets to the stadium. I need his weight if we run what you might call afoul of the law. And I owe him to say what I'm doing. This matters to him. He's got nothing else that matters."

"You and Ann Landers, babe. Everybody's trouble."

"My strength is as the strength of ten," I said, "because my heart is pure."

"What you want me to do with Paul or Zachary or whatever, case I should encounter their ass?"

"You should make a citizen's arrest."

"And if they resist, seeing as I ain't hardly a citizen of this country?"

"You'll do what you do best, Hawk."

"A man like to be recognized for his work, bawse. Thank you kindly."

"You keep the car," I said. "I'll get a cab to the airport."

I left my gun in the house. I wasn't taking any luggage and I didn't want to thrash around at customs. It was just after two in the afternoon when we swung in over Winthrop and headed in to the runway at Logan Airport, home.

I took a cab straight from the airport to Weston and at three-twenty I was ringing on Hugh Dixon's doorbell again the same way I had a month before. The same Oriental man answered the door and said, "Mr. Spenser, this way." Not bad, he'd seen me only once, a month before. Of course I suppose he was expecting me.

Dixon was on his patio, looking at the hills. The cat was there, asleep. It was like when you come back from the war and the front lawn looks just as it did and people are cooking supper and you realize they've been doing it all along, while you've been gone.

Dixon looked at me and said nothing.

"I've got your people, Mr. Dixon," I said.

"I know. Five for sure, I assume your word is good on the others. Carroll is looking into it. You want money for the first five. Carroll will pay you."

"We'll settle up later," I said. "I want to stay on this a little longer."

"At my expense?"

"No."

"Then why are you here?"

"I need some help."

"Carroll tells me you've employed some help. A black man."

"I need different help than that."

"What do you want to do? Why do you want to stay on? What help do you need?"

"I got your people for you, but while I was getting them I found out that they were only the leaves of the crabgrass. I know who the root is. I want to dig him up."

"Did he have a part in the killing?"

"Not yours, no, sir."

"Then why should I care about him?"

"Because he has had a part in a lot of other killings and because he'll probably kill somebody else's family and somebody else's after that."

"What do you want?"

"I want you to get me tickets to the Olympic games. The track and field events at the stadium. And if I get into a bind I want to be able to say I work for you."

"Tell me what's going on. Leave nothing out."

"Okay, there's a man named Paul, I don't know his last name, and possibly a man named Zachary. They run a terrorist organization called Liberty. I think they are in Montreal. I think they are going to do something rash at the Olympic games."

"Start at the beginning."

I did. Dixon looked at me steadily, without movement, without interruption, as I told him everything I had done in London and Copenhagen and Amsterdam and Montreal.

When I was through, Dixon pushed a button in the arm of his wheelchair and in a minute the Oriental man appeared.

Dixon said, "Lin, bring me five thousand dollars."

The Oriental man nodded and went out.

Dixon said to me, "I'll pay for this."

"There's no need for that," I said. "I'll pick up this one."

"No," Dixon shook his head. "I have a great deal of money and no other purpose. I'll pay for this. If the police present problems I'll do what I can to remove them. I'll have no trouble with Olympic tickets, I assume. Give your Montreal address to Lin before you leave. I'll have the tickets delivered there."

"I'll need three for every day."

"Yes."

Lin returned with fifty one-hundred-dollar bills.

"Give them to Spenser," Dixon said.

Lin handed them to me. I put them in my wallet.

Dixon said, "When this is through, come back here and tell me about it in person. If you die, have the black man do it."

"I will, sir."

"I hope you don't die," Dixon said.

"Me too," I said. "Goodbye."

Lin showed me out. I asked if he could call me a cab. He said he could. He did. I sat on a bench in the stone-paved foyer while I waited for it to come. When it came, Lin let me out. I got in the cab and said to the driver, "Take me to Smithfield."

"That's a pretty good ride, man," the cabby said. "It's gonna cost some jack."

"I got some jack."

"Okay."

We wheeled down the winding drive and out onto the road and headed toward Route 128. Smithfield was about a half-hour drive. The dashboard clock in the cab worked. It was quarter to five. She should be coming home from summer school soon, if she was still in summer school. *Oh, Susanna, oh don't you cry for me, I come from Montreal with* . . .

The cabbie said, "What'd you say, man?"

"I was singing softly to myself," I said.

"Oh, I thought you was talking to me. You want to sing to yourself, go ahead."

23

It was out of the way but I had the cabbie take me to Route 1. I stopped at Karl's Sausage Kitchen for some German delicatessen and then at Donovan's Package Store for four bottles of Dom Perignon. It almost took care of Dixon's expense money.

The cabbie drove me down from Route 1 to the center of town, through the hot green tunnel of July trees. Lawns were being watered, dogs were being called, bikes were being ridden, cookouts were being done, pools were being splashed, drinks were being had, tennis was being played. Suburbia writ large. There was some kind of barbecue underway on the common around the meeting house. The smoke from the barbecue wagons hung over the folding tables in a light good-smelling haze. There were dogs there and children and a balloon man. I did not hear him whistle far and wee. If he had, it wouldn't have been for me.

There were white lilacs in Susan's front yard, and the shingles on the little Cape were weathered into a nice silvery gray. I paid the cabbie and gave him a large tip. And he left me standing with my champagne and my homemade cold cuts on Susan's green lawn in the slow evening. Her little blue Nova was not in the driveway. The guy next door was hosing his grass, letting the water stream out of the pistol spray nozzle in a long easy loop, coiling languidly back and forth across the lawn. A sprinkler would have been much more efficient but nowhere near as much fun. I liked a man who fought off technology. He nodded at me as I went up to Susan's door. She never locked the house. I went in the front door. The house was quiet and empty. I put the champagne and the stuff from Karl's in the refrigerator. I went to the bedroom and turned on the air conditioner. It was ten past six by the clock on the kitchen stove.

I found some Utica Club cream ale in the refrigerator and opened a can while I unpacked my delicatessen in the kitchen. There was veal loaf and pepper loaf and beer wurst, and Karl's liverwurst, which you could slice or spread and which made my blood flow a little faster when I thought of it.

I had bought two cartons of German potato salad and some pickles and a loaf of Westphalian rye and a jar of Dusseldorf mustard. I got out Susan's kitchen china and set the table in the kitchen. She had blue-figured kitchen china and it always made me feel like folks to eat off it. I sliced the liverwurst and put the assorted cold cuts on a platter in alternating patterns. I put the rye bread in a bread basket and the pickles in a cut-glass dish and the potato salad in a large blue-patterned bowl that was probably intended for soup. Then I went in the dining room where she kept the company china and stuff and got two champagne glasses I had bought her for her birthday, and put them in the freezer to chill. They had cost $24.50 each. The store had felt that monogramming *His* and *Hers* on them would be ''kitsch,'' I think they said. So they were plain. But they were our glasses and they were for drinking champagne out of on special occasions. Or at least I thought they were. I was always afraid I'd come in some day and find her sprouting an avocado pit in one.

Moving about in her familiar kitchen, in her house where it seemed I could smell her perfume faintly, I felt even more strongly the sense of change and strangeness. The cookouts, the watered lawns, the weekday suburban evening coming on had that effect, and the house where she lived and read and did the dishes, where she bathed and slept and watched the *Today* show, were so real that what I'd been doing seemed unreal. I'd killed two men in a hotel in London earlier this summer. It was hard to remember. The bullet wound had healed. The men were in the ground. And here, this endured, and the man next door, watering his lawn in translucent graceful curves, didn't know anything at all about it.

I opened another can of beer and went into the bathroom and took a shower. I had to move two pairs of her panty hose that were drying on the rod that held the shower curtain. She used Ivory soap. She had some kind of fancy shampoo that came in a jar like cold cream and had a flower smell to it. I used it. Ferdinand the Bull.

There were some Puma jogging shoes, blue nylon with a white stripe, that I used sometimes when I was there for a weekend, and a pair of my white duck pants that Suze had washed and ironed and hung in a part of one of her bedroom closets that we'd come to call mine. The part, not the closet. I wore the Pumas without socks, you can do that if your ankles are good, and slipped into the ducks. I was combing my hair in her bedroom mirror when I heard the crunch of tires in her driveway. I peeked out the window. It was her.

She'd come in the back door. I hopped on the bed and lay on my left side, facing the door, head propped on my left elbow, one knee drawn seductively up. My left leg fully extended, toes pointing. The bedroom door was ajar. My heart was thumping. *Christ, is that corny,* I thought. *Heart pounding, mouth dry, breath a little short. I took one look at you, that's all I meant to do.* I heard the back door open. The silence. Then the door closed. I felt the apprehension in my solar plexus. I heard her walk through the kitchen to the living room. Then straight to the bedroom door. The air conditioning hummed. Then she was there. In tennis dress, still carrying a racket, her black hair off her face with a wide white band. Her lipstick very bright and her legs tan. The hum of the air conditioner seemed a little louder. Her face was a little flushed from tennis and a faint small gloss of sweat was on her forehead. It was the longest we had been apart since we'd met.

I said, "Home from the hills is the hunter."

"From the kitchen setup," she said, "it would appear that you'd bagged a German delicatessen." Then she put her tennis racket on the bedside table and jumped on top of me. She put both arms around my neck and kissed me on the mouth and held it. When she stopped I said, "Nice girls don't kiss with their mouths open."

She said, "Did you have an operation in Denmark? You're wearing perfume."

I said, "No. I used your shampoo."

She said, "Oh, thank heavens," and pressed her mouth on me again.

I slid my hand down her back and under the tennis dress. I'd had small experience with tennis dresses and wasn't doing well with this one.

She lifted her face from mine. "I'm all sweaty," she said.

"Even if you weren't," I said, "you would be soon."

"No," she said, "I've got to take a bath first."

"Jesus Christ," I said.

"I can't help it," she said. "I have to." Her voice was a little hoarse.

"Well, for crissake why not a shower. A bath, for God sake. I may commit a public disgrace on your stereo by the time you run a bath."

"A shower will ruin my hair."

"Do you know the ruination I face?"

"I'll be quick," she said. "I haven't seen you in a long time either."

She got up from the bed and ran the water in the bathtub off the bedroom. Then she came back in and pulled the shades and undressed. I watched her. The tennis dress had pants underneath.

"Ah ha," I said. "That's why my progress was slower than I'm used to."

"Poor thing," she said, "you've seduced a low-class clientele. With a better upbringing you'd have learned years ago how to cope with a tennis dress." She was wearing a white bra and white bikini underpants. She looked at me with that look she had, nine parts innocence and one part evil, and said, "All the guys at the club know."

"If they only knew what to do after they'd gotten the dress off," I said. "How come you wear pants under pants?"

"Only a cheap hussy would play tennis without underwear." She took off the bra.

"Or kiss with her mouth open," I said.

"Oh no," she said as she wiggled out of the underpants, "everyone at the club does that."

I'd seen her naked now enough times to stop counting. But I never lost interest. She wasn't fragile. She was strong-looking. Her stomach was flat and her breasts didn't sag. She was beautiful and she always looked a little uncomfortable naked, as if someone might burst in and say, "Ah hah!"

"Take your bath, Suze," I said. "Tomorrow I may go beat up the club."

She went into the bathroom and I could hear her splashing around in the water.

"If you're playing with a rubber ducky in there I'm going to drown you."

"Patience," she yelled. "I'm soaking in an herbal bubble bath that will drive you wild."

"I'm wild enough," I said. I took off my white ducks and my Pumas.

She came out of the bathroom with a towel tucked under her chin. It hung to her knees. With her right hand she removed it, the way you open a curtain, and said, "Tada."

"Not bad," I said. "I like a person who stays in shape."

She dropped the towel and got on the bed with me. I opened my arms and she got inside. I hugged her.

"I'm glad you're back in one piece," she said, her mouth very close to mine.

"Me too," I said, "and speaking of one piece . . ."

"Now," she said, "I'm not sweaty."

I kissed her. She pressed harder against me and I could hear her breath go in deep once through her nose and come out slowly in a long sigh. She ran her hand over my hip and down along my backside. It stopped when she felt the scar of the bullet wound.

With her lips lightly against mine she said, "What's this?"

"Bullet wound."

"I gather you weren't attacking," she said.

"I am now," I said.

And then we didn't talk.

24

"In the ass?" Susan said.

"I like to think of it as a hamstring wound," I said.

"I'll bet you do," she said. "Was it bad?"

"Undignified but not serious," I said.

We were eating deli and drinking champagne in her kitchen. I had my white ducks back on and my Pumas. She had on a bathrobe. Outside it was dark now. Nonurban night sounds drifted in through the open back door. Night insects pinged against the screen.

"Tell me. All of it. From the beginning."

I put two slices of veal loaf on some rye bread, added a small application of Dusseldorf mustard, put another slice of bread on top and bit. I chewed and swallowed.

"Two shots in the ass and I was off on the greatest adventure of my career," I said. I took a bite of half sour pickle. It clashed a little with the champagne, but life is flawed.

"Be serious," Susan said. "I want to hear about it. Have you had a bad time? You look tired."

"I am tired," I said. "I've just been screwing my brains out."

"Oh really?"

"Oh really," I said. "How come you were doing all that sighing and moaning?"

"Boredom," she said. "Those weren't sighs and moans. Those were yawns."

"Nice talk to a wounded man."

"Well," she said, "I am glad the bullet didn't go all the way through."

I poured some champagne in her glass and mine. I put the bottle down, raised the glass and said, "Here's looking at you, kid."

She smiled. The smile made me want to say *Oh boy*, but I'm too worldly to say it out loud.

"Begin at the beginning," she said. "You got on the plane after you left me and . . .?"

"And I landed in London about eight hours later. I didn't like leaving you."

"I know," she said.

"And a guy named Flanders that works for Hugh Dixon met me at the airport . . ." and I told her all, the people that tried to kill me, the people I killed, all of it.

"No wonder you look tired," she said when I finished. We were on the last bottle of champagne and most of the food was gone. She was easy to tell things to. She understood quickly, she supplied missing pieces without asking questions, and she was interested. She wanted to hear.

"What do you think about Kathie?" I said.

"She needs a master. She needs structure. When you destroyed her structure, and her master turned her out, she latched on to you. When she wanted to solidify the relationship by complete submission, which for her must be sexual, you turned her out. I would guess she'll be Hawk's as long as he'll have her. How's that for instant psychoanalysis. Just add a bottle of champagne and serve off the top of the head."

"I'd say you were right, though."

"If you report accurately, and it's something you're

good at," Susan said, "certainly she's a rigid and re-
pressed personality. The way her room was, the colorless
clothing and the flashy underwear, the tight-lipped commit-
ment to a kind of Nazi absolutism."

"Yeah, she's all of that. She's some kind of masochist.
Maybe that's not quite the right term. But when she was
tied up and gagged on the bed she liked it. Or at least it
aroused her to be tied like that and have us there. She went
crazy when Hawk searched her while she was tied."

"I'm not sure masochist is the right word. But obviously she finds some connection between sex and helplessness and helplessness and humiliation and humiliation and
pleasure. Most of us have conflicting tendencies toward
aggression and passivity. If we have healthy childhoods
and get through adolescence okay we tend to work them
out. If we don't, then we confuse them and tend to be like
Kathie, who hasn't worked out her passivity impulses."
Susan smiled. "Or you, who are quite aggressive."

"But gallant," I said.

"How do you think Hawk will deal with her?" Susan
said.

"Hawk has no feelings," I said. "But he has rules. If
she fits one of his rules, he'll treat her very well. If she
doesn't, he'll treat her any way the mood strikes him."

"Do you really think he has no feelings?"

"I have never seen any. He's as good as anyone I ever
saw at what he does. But he never seems happy or sad or
frightened or elated. He never, in the twenty-some years
I've known him, here and there, has shown any sign of
love or compassion. He's never been nervous. He's never
been mad."

"Is he as good as you?" Susan was resting her chin on
her folded hands and looking at me.

"He might be," I said. "He might be better."

"He didn't kill you last year on Cape Cod when he was supposed to. He must have felt something then."

"I think he likes me, the way he likes wine, the way he doesn't like gin. He preferred me to the guy he was working for. He sees me as a version of himself. And, somewhere in there, killing me on the say-so of a guy like Powers was in violation of one of the rules. I don't know. I wouldn't have killed him either."

"Are you a version of him?"

"I got feelings," I said. "I love."

"Yes, you do," Susan said. "And quite well too. Let us take this last bottle of champagne to the bedroom and lie down and drink it and continue the conversation and perhaps once more you would care to, as the kids at the high school say, do it."

"Suze," I said, "I'm a middle-aged man."

"I know," Susan said. "I see it as a challenge."

We went into the bedroom and lay close in the bed, sipping the champagne and watching the late movie in the air-conditioned darkness. Life may be flawed but sometimes things are just right. The late movie was *The Magnificent Seven*. When Steve McQueen looked at Eli Wallach and said, "We deal in lead, friend," I said it along with him.

"How many times have you seen this movie?" Susan asked.

"Oh, I don't know. Six, seven times, I guess. It's on a lot of late shows in hotel rooms in a lot of cities."

"How can you stand to watch it again?"

"It's like watching a dance, or listening to music. It's not plot, it's pattern."

She laughed in the darkness. "Of course it is," she said. "That's the story of your life. *What* doesn't matter. It's how you look when you do it."

"Not just how you look," I said.

"I know," she said. "My champagne is gone. Do you think you are, if you'll pardon the phrase, up for another transport of ecstasy?"

I finished the last of my champagne. "With a little help," I said, "from my friends."

She ran her hand lightly across my stomach. "I'm all the friend you've got, big fella."

"All I need," I said.

25

Next day Susan drove me to the airport. We stopped on the way in the hot bright summer morning at a Dunkin' Donut shop, and had coffee and two plain donuts apiece.

"A night of ecstasy followed by a morning of delight," I said, and bit into a donut.

"Did William Powell take Myrna Loy to a Dunkin' Donut shop?"

"He didn't know enough," I said. I raised my coffee cup toward her.

She said, "Here's looking at you, kid."

I said, "How'd you know what I was going to say?"

"Lucky guess," she said.

We were quiet on the ride to the airport. Susan was a terrible driver and I spent a lot of time stomping my right foot on the floorboards.

When she stopped at the terminal she said, "I'm getting sick of doing this. How long this time?"

"Not long," I said. "Maybe a week, no longer than the Olympic games."

"You promised me London," she said. "If you don't make it back to pay off I'll be really angry with you."

I kissed her on the mouth. She kissed me back. I said, "I love you, Suze."

She said, "I love you too," and I got out and went into the terminal.

Two hours and twenty minutes later I was back in Montreal at the house near Henri Bourassa Boulevard. It was empty. There was O'Keefe's ale in the refrigerator along with several bottles of champagne. Hawk had been shopping. I opened a bottle of O'Keefe's and sat in the living room and watched some of the games on television. At about two-thirty a man knocked at the front door. I stuck my gun in my hip pocket, just in case, and answered.

"Mr. Spenser?" The man was wearing a seersucker suit and a small-brimmed straw hat with a big blue band. He sounded American, although so did half the people in Canada. At the curb with the motor running was a Dodge Monaco with Quebec plates.

"Yeah," I said, very snappy.

"I'm from Dixon Industries. I have an envelope for you, but first could I see some ID?"

I showed him my PI license with my picture on it. I looked like one of the friends of Eddie Coyle.

"Yeah," he said, "that's you."

"It disappoints me too," I said.

He smiled automatically, gave me back my license and took a thick envelope out of his side coat pocket. It had my name on it, and the Dixon Industries logo up in the left-hand corner.

I took the envelope. The man in the seersucker suit said, "Goodbye, have a nice day," went back to his waiting Monaco, and drove off.

I went in the house and opened the envelope. It was three sets of tickets for all the events at the Olympic stadium for the duration of the games. There was nothing else. Not even a preprinted card that said HAVE A NICE DAY. The world becomes impersonal.

Hawk and Kathie returned while I was on my fourth O'Keefe's.

Hawk opened some champagne and poured a glass for Kathie and one for him. "How old Suze doing?" he asked. He sat on the couch, Kathie sat beside him. She didn't say anything.

"Fine. She said hello."

"Dixon go along?"

"Yeah. I think it gave him another purpose. Something else to think about."

"Better than watching daytime TV," Hawk said.

"You turn up anything yesterday or today?"

He shook his head. "Me and Kathie been looking, but we haven't seen anyone she know. Stadium's big. We haven't looked at it all yet."

"You scalp some tickets?"

Hawk smiled. "Yeah. Hated to. But it's your bread. Been my bread I might have taken them away. Hate scalpers."

"Yeah. How's the security?"

Hawk shrugged. "Tight, but you know. How you gonna be airtight with seventy, eighty thousand people walking in and out two, three times a day. There's a lot of buttons around, but if I wanted to do somebody in there, I could. No sweat."

"And get out?"

"Sure, with a little luck. It's a big place, man. Lot of people."

"Well, tomorrow I'll see. I got us all tickets so we don't have to deal with the scalpers."

"All *right*," Hawk said.

"Hate corruption in all its aspects, don't you, Hawk."

"Been fighting it all my life, bawse." Hawk drank some more champagne. Kathie filled his glass as soon as he put it down. She sat so that her thigh touched his and watched him all the time.

I drank some ale. "Been enjoying the games, Kath?"

She nodded without looking at me.

Hawk grinned at me. "She don't like you," he said. "She say you ain't much of a man. Say you weak, you soft, say her and me we should shake you. I getting the feeling she don't care for you. She think you a degenerate."

"I got a real way with the broads," I said.

Kathie reddened but was silent, still looking at Hawk.

"I told her she was a little hasty in her judgment."

"She believe you?"

"No. You buy anything besides booze, like for supper?"

"Naw, man, you was telling me about a place called Bacco's. Figured you'd like to take me and Kath out and show her you ain't no degenerate. Treat her to a fine meal. Me too."

"Yeah," I said. "Okay. Let me take a shower."

"See that, Kath," Hawk said. "He very clean."

Bacco's was on the second floor in the old section of Montreal not far from Victoria Square. The cuisine was French Canadian and they had one of the better country pâtés that I'd eaten. It also had good French bread and Labatt 50 ale. Hawk and I had a very nice time. I was thinking that Kathie probably did not have nice times. Ever. But she was passive and polite while we ate. She'd bought a kind of dungaree suit with a vest and long coat that she was wearing, and her hair was neat and she looked good.

Old Montreal was jumping during the Olympics. There was outdoor entertainment in a square nearby, and throngs of young people drinking beer and wine and smoking and listening to the rock music.

We got in our rented car and drove back to our rented house. Hawk and Kathie went upstairs to what had become their room. I sat for a while and finished the O'Keefe's and watched the evening events, wrestling and some of the weightlifting, alone in the rented living room, on the funny old TV set with the illuminated border.

At nine o'clock I went to bed. Alone. I hadn't had much sleep the night before and I was tired. I felt middle-aged. I was lonely. It kept me awake till nine-fifteen.

26

We took the subway to the Olympic Stadium. Subway is probably the wrong term. If what I ride occasionally in Boston is a subway, then what we rode in Montreal was not. The stations were immaculate, the trains silent, the service on time. Hawk and I forced a small space for Kathie between us, in the jam of bodies. We changed at Berri Montigny and got off at Viau.

Being a supercool sophisticated worldly-wise full-grown hipster, I was unimpressed with the enormous complex around the Olympic Stadium. Just as I was unimpressed with going to the actual, real, live Olympic games. The excited circus feeling in my stomach was merely the man-hunter's natural sensation as he closes in on his quarry. Straight ahead were food pavilions and concessions of one kind or another. Beyond was the Maisonneuve Sports Center, to my right the Maurice Richard Arena, to my left the Velodrome and, beyond it, looming like the Colosseum, the gray, not quite finished, monumental stadium. Cheering surged up from it. We started up the long winding ramp toward the stadium. As we went I sucked in my stomach.

Hawk said, "Kathie say this Zachary a bone-breaker."

"How big is he?"

Hawk said, "Kath?"

"Very big," she said.

"Bigger than me," I said, "or Hawk?"

"Oh yes. I mean really big."

"I weigh about two hundred pounds," I said. "How much would you say he weighs?"

"He weighs three hundred five pounds. I know. I heard him tell Paul one day."

I looked at Hawk. "Three hundred five?"

"But he only six feet seven," Hawk said.

"Is he fat, Kathie?" I was hopeful.

"No, not really. He used to be a weightlifter."

"Well, so, Hawk and I do a lot on the irons."

"No, I mean like those Russians. You know, a real weightlifter, he was the champion of somewhere."

"And he looks like a Russian weightlifter?"

"Yes, like that. Paul and he used to watch them on television. He has that fat look that you know is strong."

"Well, anyway, he won't be hard to spot."

"Harder here than most places," Hawk said.

"Yeah. Let's be careful and not try to put the arm on Alexeev or somebody."

Hawk said, "This dude trying to save Africa too?"

"Yes. He . . . he hates blacks worse than anyone I've seen."

"That helps," I said. "You can reason with him, Hawk."

"I got something under my coat for reasoning."

"If we run into him we're going to have trouble shooting. There's too many people."

"You think we should wrestle him, maybe?" Hawk said. "You and me good, babe, but we ain't used to no giants. And we got that other mean little sucker we got to think of."

We were at the gate. We handed in our tickets and then we were inside. There were several tiers. Our tickets were for tier one. I could hear the crowd roaring inside now. I was dying to see.

I said, "Hawk, you and Kathie start circling that way, and I'll go this way. We'll start at the first level and work up. Be careful. Don't let Paul spot you first."

"Or old Zach," Hawk said. "I be especially careful about Zach."

"Yeah. We'll keep working up to the top tier, then start back down again. If you spot them, stay with them. We'll eventually intersect again as long as we stay in the stadium."

Hawk and Kathie started off. "If you see Zachary," Hawk said over his shoulder, "and you want to do him in, it okay. You don't have to wait for me. You free to take him right there."

"Thanks," I said. "I think you ought to have a shot at the racist bastard."

Hawk went off with Kathie. He seemed to glide. I wasn't so sure he couldn't handle Zachary. I went off the other way, trying to glide. I seemed to be doing pretty well. Maybe I could manage Zachary too. I was as ready as I was going to be. Pale blue Levis, white polo shirt, blue suede Adidas with three white stripes, a blue blazer and a plaid cap for disguise. The blazer didn't go but it provided cover for the gun on my hip. I was tempted to limp a little so people would think I was a competitor, temporarily out of action. Decathlon maybe. No one seemed to be paying me any attention so I didn't bother. I went up the ramp to the first-level seating. It was better than I had imagined. The stadium seats were colorful, yellow and blue and such, and when I came out of the passageway there was a bright blaze of color. Below the stadium floor was bright green grass, ringed with red running track. Directly below me and near the side of the stadium, girls were doing the long jump. They had on white tops mostly, with large numbers affixed, and very high-cut tight shorts. The electronic scorekeeper was to my left near the pit where the jump finished. Judges in yellow blazers were at the start point, the take-off line, and the pit. A girl from West Germany started down the track in that peculiar long-gaited stride that long jumpers have, nearly straight-legged. She fouled at the take-off line.

In the middle of the stadium, men were throwing the discus. They all looked like Zachary. An African discus thrower had just launched one. It didn't look very good, and it looked even worse a minute later when a Pole threw one far beyond it.

Around the stadium there were athletes in colorful sweat clothes, jogging and stretching, loosening up and staying warm and doing what jocks always do waiting for an event. They moved and massaged muscles and bounced and shrugged.

At either end of the stadium, at the top, were scoreboards, one at each end, with instant replay mechanism. I watched the Pole's huge discus toss again.

"The goddamned Olympics," I said to myself. "Jesus Christ."

I hadn't thought much about going to the games until I got off the subway. I'd been busy with the business at hand. But now that I was here looking down on the actual event, a sense of such strangeness and excitement came over me that I forgot about Zachary and Paul and the deaths at Munich and stared down at the Olympics, thinking of Melbourne and Rome and Tokyo and Mexico City and Munich, of Wilma Rudolph, and Jesse Owens, Bob Mathias, Rafer Johnson, Mark Spitz, Bill Toomey, the names flooded back at me. Cassius Clay, Emil Zatopek, the clenched fists at Mexico City, Alexeev Cathy Rigby, Tenley Albright. Wow.

An usher said, "You seated, sir?"

"That's okay," I said. "It's over there, I just wanted to stop here a minute before I went on."

"Of course, sir," he said.

I started looking for Paul. I was wearing sunglasses, and I tipped the hat down over my forehead. Paul wouldn't expect to see me, if he were here, and Zachary didn't know me. I looked section by section, starting at the first row and moving up and down the rows slowly, one row at a time, up to the end of the section. Then I moved on. It was hard to concentrate and not begin to skim over the faces. But I concentrated and tried to pay no attention to the games right there below me. It was an outdoor sports crowd, well-dressed and able to afford the Olympic tickets. Lots of kids and cameras and binoculars. Across the stadium a group of male sprinters gathered for a 100-meter heat. I picked out the American colors. I discovered that I wanted the American to win. Son of a bitch. A patriot. A nationalist. The PA system made a little chiming sound and then an announcer said, first in French, then in English, that the qualifying heat was about to begin.

I kept drifting through the stands looking up and down the rows. A lot of Americans. The starting gun cracked across the stadium and the runners broke out of the blocks. I stopped and watched. The American won. He jogged on around the track, a tall black kid with that runner's bounce, with USA on his shirt. I looked some more. It was like at a ball game, but the crowd was more affluent, more dignified, and the events below were of a different order. A vendor moved by me selling Coke.

On the field below, a platoon of Olympic officials in Olympic blazers marched out onto the near side track and picked up the long jump paraphernalia. And took it away. An American threw the discus. Farther than the African.

Not as far as the Pole. I circled the whole stadium, getting tired of looking, stopping now and then to watch the games. I saw Hawk and Kathie two sections over, she was holding his arm, he was doing what I was doing. I started around again and I stopped at the second level for beer and a hot dog.

I put mustard and relish on the hot dog, took a sip of beer, a bite of hot dog (it was so-so, not Olympian) and looked out through the runway to the stands. Paul came down the runway. I turned back toward the counter and ate some more of my hot dog. A tribute to careful search and survey techniques and a masterpiece of concentration, looking over the stands aisle by aisle, and he almost walks into me while I'm eating a hot dog. Super sleuth.

Paul moved on past me without looking and headed up the ramp toward level three. I finished the hot dog and drank the beer and drifted along behind him. I didn't see anyone who looked like Zachary. I didn't mind.

At the third deck Paul went to a spot in the runway and looked down at the stadium floor. I went in the next ramp and watched him across the seats. The athletes looked smaller up here. But just as poised and just as agile. The squad of officials was breaking out low hurdles as we looked down at them. The discus throwers were leaving and the officials for that event formed into a small phalanx and marched out. Paul looked around, glanced up at the top of the stadium and back into the runway behind him. I stayed half inside my runway, a section away, and watched him sideways behind my sunglasses underneath my plaid cap.

Paul came back up the runway and turned down along the ramp that ran beneath the stands. I followed. There was a large kiosk where the washroom was located, and between it and the wall beneath the stands there was a narrow space. Paul stood looking at the space. I leaned on the wall and read a program, across the width of the ramp by a support pillar. Paul walked through the space beyond the washroom and into another ramp, then he came back up the ramp and stood in the space beyond the washroom staring down toward the ramp.

There wasn't much activity under the stands, and I stayed back of the post with just a slot between it and the edge of the washroom kiosk to see. I was okay as long as Hawk didn't show up with Kathie and run into Paul. If he did we'd take him right there, but I wanted to see what he'd do. He glanced over his shoulder back toward the washroom. No one came out. He leaned against the wall at the corner and took out what looked like a spyglass. He aimed the spyglass down the ramp, leaning it against the corner of the kiosk. He adjusted the focus, raised and lowered a little, then took a large Magic Marker and drew a small black stripe under the spyglass, holding the spyglass like a straight edge against the building. He put the Magic Marker away, sighted the spyglass again by holding it against the line on the wall, and then collapsed it and slipped it away in his pocket. Without looking around he went in the men's room.

Maybe three minutes later he came out. It was noon. The morning games were ending and the crowd began to pour out. From almost empty, the corridors under the stands became jammed. I forced after Paul and stayed with him to the subway. But as the train for Berri Montigny pulled out of Viau I was standing three rows back on the boarding platform calling the man in front of me an asshole.

27

By the time I got back to the stadium it had cleared. Ticket holders for the afternoon games would not be admitted for an hour. I hung around the entrance marked for our ticket section and Hawk showed up in five minutes. Kathie wasn't holding his arm. She was walking a little behind him. When he saw me he shook his head.

I said, "I saw him."

"He alone?"

"Yeah. I lost him, though, in the subway."

"Shit."

"He'll be back. He was marking out a position up on the second deck. This afternoon we'll go take a look at it."

Kathie said to Hawk, "Can we eat?"

"Want to try the Brasserie down there?" Hawk said to me.

"Yeah."

We moved down toward the open area before the station stairs near the Sports Center. There were small hot-dog and hamburg stands, souvenir stands, a place to buy coins and stamps, a washroom, and a big festive-looking tent complex with the sides open and banners flying from the tent-pole peaks. Inside were big wooden tables and benches. Waiters and waitresses circulated, taking orders and bringing food and drink.

We ate, beer and sausage, and watched the excited people eating at the other tables. A lot of Americans. More than anything else, maybe more than Canadians. Kathie went to stand in the line at the ladies' room. Hawk and I had a second beer.

"What you figure?" Hawk said.

"I don't know. I'd guess he's got a shooting stand marked. He was looking through a telescope and marked a spot on the wall at shoulder level. I'd like to get a look at what you can see from that spot."

Kathie came back. We walked back up toward the stadium. The afternoon crowd was beginning to go in. We went in with them and went right to the second level. On the wall by the corner of the washroom near the entry ramp was Paul's mark. Before we went to it we circled around the area. No sign of Paul.

We looked at the mark. If you sighted along it, pressing your cheek against the wall, you would look straight down into the stadium at the far side of the infield, this side of the running track. There was nothing there now but grass. Hawk took a look.

"Why here?" he said.

"Maybe the only semi-concealed place with a shot at the action."

"Then why the mark? He can remember where it is."

"Must be something here. In that spot. If you were going to burn somebody for effect at the Olympic games, what would you choose?"

"The medals."

"Yeah. Me too. I wonder if the awards ceremonies take place down there?"

"Haven't seen one. There ain't many at the beginning of the games."

"We'll watch."

And we did. I watched the mark and Hawk circulated through the stadium with Kathie. Paul didn't reappear. No medals were awarded. But the next day they were, and looking down along Paul's mark on the washroom wall I could see the three white boxes and the gold medalist in the discus standing on the middle one.

"Okay," I said to Hawk. "We know what he's going to do. Now we have to hang around and catch him when."

"How you know he ain't got half a dozen marks like this all over the stadium?"

"I don't but I figured you'd keep looking for them and if you didn't see any we could count on this one."

"Yeah. You stay on this one, Kathie and me we keep circulating. Program say there's no more finals today. So I guess he ain't gonna do it today."

And he didn't. And he didn't the next day, but the next day he showed and he brought Zachary with him.

Zachary was nowhere near as big as an elephant. In fact he wasn't much bigger than a Belgian draught horse. He had a blond crew cut and a low forehead. He wore a blue-and-white striped sleeveless tank top jersey and knee-length plaid Bermuda shorts. I was staked out by the shooting mark when they arrived and Hawk was circulating with Kathie.

Paul, carrying a blue equipment bag with OLYMPIQUE MONTREAL, 1976 stenciled on the side, checked his watch, put the equipment bag down, took out a small telescope and sighted along his mark. Zachary folded his incredible arms across his monumental chest and leaned against the side of the washroom wall, shielding Paul. Behind Zachary, Paul knelt and opened his bag. Down the curve of the stadium ramp I could see Hawk and Kathie appear. I didn't want them spotted. Paul wasn't looking and Zachary didn't know me. I stepped out from my alcove behind the pillar and strolled on down toward Hawk. When he saw me coming he stopped and moved against the wall. When I reached them he said, "They here?"

"Yeah, up by the mark. Zachary too."

"How you know it's Zachary for sure?"

"It's either Zachary or there's a whale loose in the stands."

"Big as she said, huh?"

"At least that big," I said. "You're going to love him."

From inside the stadium came a sound of chimes and then the PA speaker's voice in French.

"Awards ceremony," Hawk said.

"Okay," I said. "We gotta do it now." We moved, Kathie behind us.

Around the corner, behind Zachary, Paul had assembled a rifle, with a scope. I brought my gun out of my hip holster and said, "Hold it right there." Clever. Hawk had the cutdown shotgun out and level.

He looked at Zachary and said, "Shit," stretching the word into two syllables.

Zachary had a small automatic pistol in his hand, hidden against his thigh. He raised it as I spoke. Paul whirled with the sniper rifle level and all four of us froze there. Three women and two children came out of the washroom and stopped. One of the women said, "Oh my god."

Kathie came around the other corner of the washroom kiosk and began to hit Paul in the face with both hands. He slapped her away with the rifle barrel. The three women and their daughters were screaming now and trying to get out of the way, and some other people appeared. I said to Hawk, "Don't shoot."

He nodded, reversed his hands on the shotgun and swung it like a baseball bat. He hit Paul across the base of the skull with the stock of the shotgun, and Paul went down without a sound. Zachary fired at me and missed, and I chopped at his gun hand with the barrel of my gun. I missed, but it caused him to jerk his arm and he missed again at close range. I tried to get my gun up against him so I could shoot without hitting anyone else, and he twisted it away from me with his left hand and it clattered on the floor. I grabbed onto his right with both hands and pushed the gun away from me.

Hawk hit him with the shotgun but Zachary hunched his shoulders and Hawk hit him too low, catching the massed-up trapezius muscles. While I hung onto his right arm Zachary half spun and caught Hawk with the left arm, like the boom coming across on a sailboat, and sent him and the shotgun in different directions. While he was distracted I was able to get his grip loosened on the pistol. It was the strength of both my hands against his fingers and I almost lost. I twisted his forefinger back as hard as I could and the automatic hit the cement floor.

Zachary grunted and folded me in against him with his right arm. He brought the left one around too, but before he could close it around me Hawk was back up and got hold of it. I butted Zachary under the nose and then twisted down and away. He flung Hawk from him again, and as he did I rolled away from him and back up on my feet.

There were a lot of people around now and I heard someone yelling about police and there was a kind of murmurous babble of fright in different languages. Zachary had backed a couple of steps away from us, against the wall, Hawk was to his right and I was to his left in a ring of people milling about. Zachary's breath was heavy and there was sweat on his face. To my right I could see Hawk moving into the boxer's shuffle that I'd seen him use before. There was a bruise swelling along the cheekbone under his right eye. His face was shiny and bright and he was smiling. His breath was quiet, and his hands moved slightly in front of him, chest-high. He was whistling almost inaudibly through his teeth, "Do Nothing Till You Hear from Me."

Zachary looked at Hawk, then at me. I realized I was in almost the same stance Hawk was in. Zachary looked back at Hawk. At me. At Hawk. Time was with us. If we held him there, in a little while there would be cops and guns and he knew it. He looked at me again. Then took a breath.

"Hawk," I said. And Zachary charged. Hawk and I both grabbed at him and bounced off, Hawk from his right shoulder, me off his left thigh. I had tried to get low but he was quicker than he should have been and I didn't get down low enough fast enough. The milling crowd scattered like pigeons, swooping aside and settling back as Zachary burst through them, heading for the ramp. I tasted blood in my mouth as I got up, and Hawk's nose seemed to be bleeding.

We went after Zachary. He was pounding down the ramp ahead of us. Hawk said to me, "We can catch him okay, but what we gonna do with him?"

"No more Mr. Nice Guy," I said. My lip was puffing and it was hard to speak clearly. We were out of the stadium now, past two startled ushers and running along the outside terrace that led down to the eating and concession areas.

Zachary went down the stairs two at a time at the end of the terrace. He was agile and very fast for a guy the size of a drive-in movie. He cut left at the bottom of the stairs toward the swimming and diving building. I put a hand on the railing and vaulted over the retaining wall and landed on him eight feet below. My weight hitting him made him stumble forward, and we both sprawled on the concrete. I had one hand locked around his neck as we hit, but he rolled over on top of me and tore loose. Hawk came around the corner of the stairs and kicked Zachary in the side of the head as he started to get up. It didn't stop him. He was on his feet and running. Hawk hit him with a right hook in the throat and Zachary grunted and ran over Hawk and kept going. Hawk and I looked at each other on the ground. I said, "You may have to turn in your big red S."

"He can run," Hawk said, "but he can't hide," and we went after him. Past the swimming arena Zachary turned right up a long steady hill toward the park that spread out around that end of the stadium complex.

"The hill's gonna kill him," I said to Hawk.

"Ain't doing me that goddamned much good either," Hawk said. But his breathing was still easy and he still moved like a series of springs.

"Three hundred pounds moving uphill is going to hurt. He'll be tired when we catch him."

Ahead of us Zachary churned on. Even at fifty yards we could see the sweat soaked through his striped shirt. Mine was wet too. I glanced down as I ran. It was wet with blood that must be running from my cut lip. I looked at Hawk.. The lower half of his face was covered with blood and his shirt was spattered too. One eye had started to close.

We began to close. All the years of jogging, three, four, five miles a day, was staying with me. The legs felt good, my breath was coming easy and as the sweat began to come it seemed to make everything go smoother. There weren't many people here. And the ones we saw didn't register. The running got hypnotic as we pressed after Zachary. A steady rhythm of our feet, the swing of our arms, Hawk's feet were almost soundless as they hit the ground going up the long hill. Near the top we were right behind Zachary and at the top he stopped, his chest heaving, his breath rasping in his damaged throat, the sweat running on his face. Slightly ahead of us, slightly above, with the sun behind him, he stood and waited, high and huge, as if he had risen on his hind legs. We had bayed him.

28

Hawk and I slowed and stopped about five feet away. Two athletes, a man and a woman, were jogging and they stopped a short distance away and stared.

Hawk moved to Zachary's right. Zachary turned slightly toward him, I moved a little more to his left. He turned back. Hawk moved closer. He turned slightly toward Hawk and I edged in. Zachary made a grunting sound. Maybe he was trying to speak. But it came out a kind of snarling grunt. He took a step toward me and Hawk stepped in and hit him again in the throat.

Zachary croaked and swung at Hawk. Hawk had moved out of reach and I was inside of Zachary's arm hitting him in the body, left, right, left, right. It was like working on the heavy bag. He croaked again and squeezed his arms around me. When he did, Hawk was behind him, hitting him in the kidneys, left hook, right hook, the punches thudded home without any seeming effect. He squeezed harder. He was going to do me in, then turn at Hawk. I chopped both hands in along the edge of his jawline, where his head joined his neck. He squeezed harder. I was beginning to see spots. I put both hands under his chin and pressed my back against his grasp, pushing his head back very slowly. Hawk stepped around and, one finger at a time, began to pry his hands loose from each other. The grip broke, and I pushed free.

Hawk hit him with a combination left jab, right hook right on the chin. It snapped Zachary's head back but that's all. Hawk stepped out away from Zachary, shaking his right hand. As he did, Zachary caught him with the back of his right hand and Hawk went down.

I kicked Zachary in the groin. He half turned and I half missed, but he grunted with the pain. Hawk scrambled away and got to his feet. He was covered with blood and so was Zachary. We were all bleeding now and smeared with each other's blood. Zachary was breathing hard. He seemed to be having trouble, as if his throat were closing where Hawk had caught him earlier. In the distance was a siren but no one was where we were.

Hawk circled in at Zachary, bobbing a little. "Nigger," Zachary rasped. He spit at Hawk. I circled the other way. We kept narrowing the circle. Finally we were too close. Zachary got hold of Hawk. I jumped on Zachary's back and tried to set a full nelson. He was too big and too strong. He broke it on me before I could set it, but Hawk got loose and pounded two more punches into Zachary's throat. Zachary grunted in pain.

I was still on his back. We were both slippery with sweat now, and blood, and rancid with body odor and exhaustion. I got one arm partly under his chin but I couldn't raise it. He reached behind him with his right arm and grabbed me by the shirt. Hawk hit him again, twice in the throat, and the pain was real. I could feel the tremor in his body, and the croak was more anguished. We were making progress.

He hauled me up over his shoulder with one arm, got his hand inside my thigh and threw me into Hawk. We both went down and Zachary came at us kicking. He got me in the ribs and I saw the spots again. Then I was up and Hawk was up and we were moving in our slow circle. Zachary's chest heaved as he dragged air in. In front of my eyes, exhaustion miasma danced. Hawk spit out a tooth. The siren was louder.

Hawk said, "We don't do him in soon, cops will be here."

"I know," I said, and moved in on Zachary again. He swung at me massively, but slow. He was tired. And was having trouble breathing. I ducked under the arm and hit him in the stomach. He chopped down on me with his fist but missed again, and Hawk hit him again in the kidneys. Hard expert punches. Zachary groaned. He turned at Hawk, but slowly, ponderously, like the last lurch of a broken machine.

I hit him in the neck behind the ear, not boxing now, throwing my fist like a sling from as far back as I could pull it, letting my whole two hundred pounds go into the punch. We had him now and I wanted to end it. He staggered, he half turned back. Hawk hit him as I had, haymaker right-hand punches, and he staggered again. I stepped in close and hit him again in the solar plexus, right, left, right, and Hawk caught him from behind with first his left elbow, then his right forearm, delivered in swinging sequence against the back of Zachary's neck. He turned again, and swinging his arm like a tree limb he knocked Hawk sprawling.

Then he lurched at me. I put two left jabs on his nose but he got hold of me with his left hand. He held me by the shirtfront and began to club me with his right fist. I covered up, pulling my head down inside my shoulders as far as I could, keeping my arms beside my head, elbows covering my body. It didn't help much. I felt something break in my left forearm. I didn't hurt much, just a snap. And I knew a bone had broken.

I drove the side of my right fist into his windpipe as hard as I could and brought my forearm around and hit Zachary along the jawline. He gasped. Then Hawk was behind Zachary and kicked him with the side of his foot in the small of his back. He bent back, half turned, and Hawk hit him a rolling, lunging right hand on the jaw, and Zachary loosened his grip on me and his knees buckled and he fell forward on his face on the ground. I stepped out of the way as he fell.

Hawk was swaying slightly as he stood on the other side of Zachary's fallen body. His face and chest and arms were covered with blood and sweat, his upper lip was swollen so badly that the pink inside showed. His right eye was closed. His sunglasses were gone and much of his shirt was shredded. One sleeve was gone entirely. A part of his lower lip moved and I think he was trying to smile. He looked down at Zachary and tried to spit. A little bloody saliva trickled on his chin. He said, "Honkie."

My left arm was bent a funny way above the wrist: It still didn't hurt much but my hand twitched and jumped involuntarily and I knew it was going to hurt. The front of my shirt was gone. My chest was covered with blood. My nose felt like it was broken too. That would make six times. I stepped toward Hawk and staggered. I realized I was weaving like he was.

A Montreal police car, with the light flashing and siren whooping, came up the road toward us. Several people were pointing up in our direction, running toward the car. The car came to a skidding halt and two cops rolled out of it, guns in hand.

Hawk said to me, "Didn't need no fucking cops, babe."

I put my right hand out, palm up. It was shaking. Hawk

slapped his down limply on it. We were too tired to shake. We simply clutched hands, swaying back and forth with Zachary motionless on the ground in front of us.

"Didn't need no jive-fucking cops, babe," Hawk said again, and a noise came hoarscly out of his throat. I realized he was laughing. I started to laugh too. The two Montreal cops stood looking at us with the guns half raised and the doors of the cruiser swung open. Down the hill another cop car was coming.

One of them said, "Qu'est-ce que c'est?"

"Je parle anglais," I said with the blood running off me. Laughing and gasping for breath. "Je suis Americain, mon gendarme."

Hawk was nearly hysterical with laughter. Now his body was rocking back and forth, hanging on to my good hand.

"What the hell are you doing?" the cop said.

Trying to control his laugher, Hawk said, "We just copped the gold medal in outdoor scuffling." It was the funniest thing I'd ever heard, or so it seemed at the time, and the two of us were still giggling when they loaded us into the car and hauled us off to a hospital.

29

They set my arm and packed my nose and cleaned me up, and put me in the hospital overnight with Hawk in the next bed. They didn't arrest us, but there was a cop at the door all night. My arm was hurting now and they gave me a shot. I went to sleep for the rest of the day and night. When I woke up, a man in plain clothes was there from the RCMP. Hawk was sitting up in bed reading the *Montreal Star* and sipping some juice from a big styrofoam cup through a straw from one corner of his mouth. The swelling was down a bit in his eye. He could see out of it, but the lip was still very puffy and I could see the black thread from the stitches.

"My name's Morgan," the man from RCMP said. He showed me his shield. "We'd like to hear about what happened."

Hawk said, with difficulty, "Paul dead. Kathie shot him with the rifle while he trying to escape."

"Escape?" I said.

Hawk said, "Yeah." There was no expression on his face.

"Where is she now?"

Morgan said, "We're holding her for the moment."

I said, "How's Zachary?"

Morgan said, "He'll live. We have looked into him a bit. He's in our files, in fact."

"I'll bet he is," I said. I shifted a little in bed. It hurt. I was sore all over. My left arm was in a cast from knuckles to elbow. The cast felt warm. There was tape over my nose and the nostrils were packed.

"Naturally with the games established in Montreal we kept a file of known terrorists. Zachary was quite well known. Several countries want him. What business were you doing with him?"

"We were preventing him from shooting a gold medalist. Him and Paul."

Morgan was a strong-looking middle-sized man with thick blondish hair and a thick mustache. His jaw stuck out and his mouth receded. The mustache helped. He wore rimless glasses. I hadn't seen those for years. The principal of my elementary school had worn rimless glasses.

"We rather figured that out from the witnesses and what Kathie told us. That doesn't appear, incidentally, to be her real name."

"I know. I don't know what it is."

Morgan looked at Hawk, "You?"

Hawk said, "I don't know."

Morgan looked back at me, "Anyway the rifle with the scope, the mark on the wall, that sort of thing. We were able to figure out pretty well what the plan had been. What we're interested in is a bit of information on how you happened to be there at the proper time and place. There were quite a number of weapons at the scene. None of you seemed able to hang on. There was a thirty-eight caliber Smith and Wesson revolver for which you have a permit, Mr. Spenser. And there was a modified shotgun, which is illegal in Canada, for which there is no permit, but for which your companion seems to have had a shoulder rig."

Hawk looked at the ceiling and shrugged. I didn't say anything.

"The other guns," Morgan went on, "doubtless belonged to this Paul, and to Zachary."

I said, "Yeah."

Morgan said, "Let us not bullshit around anymore. You are not tourists, either of you. Spenser, I have already checked you out. Your investigator's license was in your wallet. We called Boston and have talked about you. This gentleman," he nodded at Hawk, "admits only to being called Hawk. He carries no identification. The Boston Police, however, suggested that a man of that description who used that name was sometimes know to associate with you. They described him, I believe, as a leg-breaker. It was not a pair of tourists who took Mr. Zachary, either. Tell me. I want to hear."

I said, "I want to make a phone call."

Morgan said, "Spenser, this is not a James Cagney movie."

I said, "I want to call my employer. He has a right to some anonymity and the right to be consulted before I violate it. If I violate it."

Morgan nodded his head at the phone on the bedside table. I called Jason Carroll. He was in. I had the feeling he was always in. Always at the alert for a call from Dixon.

I said, "This is Spenser. Don't mention the name of my client and yours, but I have finished what we agreed I'd do and the cops are involved and they are asking questions."

Carroll said, "I think our client will not approve of that. Are you at your Montreal address?"

"No. I'm in the hospital." The number was on the phone and I read it off to him.

"Are you badly hurt?"

"No. I'll be out today."

"I will call our client. Then I will be in touch."

I hung up. "I have no desire to be a pain in the ass," I said to Morgan. "Just give me a few hours till I talk with my client. Go out, have lunch, come back. We cleaned up something for you. We prevented a very bad scene for you."

Morgan nodded. "I know that. We are treating you very nicely," he said. "You've had experience with the police. We don't have to be this nice."

From the next bed Hawk said, "Haw."

I said, "True. Give me a few hours till I hear from my client."

Morgan nodded again. "Yes. Certainly. I'll be back before dinner." He smiled. "There will be an officer outside your door if you need anything."

"He got on a bright red coat?" Hawk said.

"Just for formal occasions," Morgan said. "For the Queen, yes. Not for you."

He left. I said to Hawk, "You really think she shot him trying to escape?"

Hawk said, "Hell no. The minute we took off after Zachary she picked up the rifle and shot him. You know goddamned well that's what she did."

"Yeah, that's my guess."

"I don't think they know different, though. Morgan don't look dumb but he got nobody to swear it wasn't like she telling it, I think. I bet everybody looking at you and me and old lovable Zach, when she done it."

"Yeah," I said. "I think that too."

Three hours and fifteen minutes later, the door opened and Hugh Dixon came in in a motor-driven wheel chair and stopped beside my bed.

I said, "I did not expect to see you here."

He said, "I did not expect to see *you here*."

"It's not bad, I've had worse." I gestured at the next bed. "This is Hawk," I said. "This is Hugh Dixon."

Hawk said, "How do you do."

Dixon nodded his head once, without speaking. Behind him in the doorway was the Oriental man who had opened doors for me the last two times. A couple of nurses looked in through the half open door. Dixon looked at me some more.

"In a way it's too bad," he said. "Now I have nothing."

"I know," I said.

"But that's not your fault. You did what you said you'd do. My people have verified everyone. I understand they have the last one in jail here."

I shook my head. "Nope. She's not in it. I missed the last one."

Hawk looked over at me without saying anything. Dixon looked at me a long time.

I said, "How'd you get here so fast?"

"Private plane," Dixon said, "Lear jet. She's not the one?"

"No, sir," I said. "I missed the girl."

He looked at me some more. "All right. I'll pay you the full sum anyway." He took an envelope from his inside pocket and handed it to me. I didn't open it. "I've sent Carroll to the police," Dixon said. "There should be no difficulty for you. I have some influence in Canada."

"Get the girl out too," I said.

Again he looked at me. I could almost feel the weight of his look. Then he nodded. Once. "I will," he said. We were silent then, except for a faint whirr from his wheel chair.

"Carroll will take care of your medical bills," Dixon said.

"Thank you," I said.

"Thank you," Dixon said. "You did everything I wanted done. I am proud to have known you." He put out his hand. We shook hands. He rolled the chair over to Hawk and shook hands with him. He said to us both, "You are good men. If you need help from me at any time I will give it to you." Then he turned the chair and went out. The Oriental man closed the door behind him and Hawk and I were alone in the room. I opened the envelope. The check was for fifty thousand dollars.

I said to Hawk, "He doubled the fee. I'll give you half."

Hawk said, "Nope. I'll take what I signed up for."

We were quiet. Hawk said, "You gonna let that little psycho loose?"

"Yeah."

"Sentimental, dumb. You don't owe her nothing."

"She was a Judas goat but she was my Judas goat," I said. "I don't want to send her into the slaughter house too. Maybe she can stay with you."

Hawk looked at me and said again, "Haw."

"Okay, it was just a thought."

"She belong in the joint," Hawk said. "Or in the funny farm."

"Yeah, probably. But I'm not going to put her there."

"Somebody will."

"Yeah."

"And she might do somebody in 'fore they do."

"Yeah."

"You crazy, Spenser. You know that. You crazy."

"Yeah."

30

The Thames was glistening and firm below us as Susan and I stood on Westminster Bridge. My left arm was still in a cast and I was wearing my classic blue blazer with four brass buttons on the cuff, draped over my shoulders like David Niven. I could get the cast through my shirt sleeve but not through the coat. Susan had on a white dress with dark blue polka dots all over it. She had a wide white belt around her waist and white sling high-heeled shoes. Her bare arms were tan and her black hair glistened in the English twilight. We were leaning on the railing looking down at the water. I wasn't wearing a gun. I could smell her perfume.

"Ah," I said, "this sceptered isle, this England."

Susan turned her face toward me, her eyes invisible behind her enormous opaque sunglasses. There were faint parenthetical smile lines at her mouth and they deepened as she looked at me.

"We have been here for about three hours," she said. "You have sung 'A Foggy Day in London Town,' 'A Nightingale Sang in Berkeley Square,' 'England Swings Like a Pendulum Do,' 'There'll Be Blue Birds Over the White Cliffs of Dover.' You have quoted Samuel Johnson, Chaucer, Dickens and Shakespeare."

"True," I said. "I also assaulted you in the shower at the hotel."

"Yes."

"Where would you like to eat dinner?"

"You say," she said.

"Post Office Tower."

"Isn't that kind of touristy?"

"What are we, residents?"

"You're right. The tower it is."

"Want to walk?"

"Is it far?"

"Yes."

"Not in these shoes, then."

"Okay, we'll take a cab. I got a lot of bread. Stick with me, babe, and you'll be wearing ermine."

I gestured to a cab. He stopped. We climbed in and I gave him the address.

"Hawk wouldn't take half the money?" Susan said. In the cab she rested her hand lightly on my leg. Would the driver notice if I assaulted her in the cab? Probably.

I said, "Nope. He gave me a bill for his expenses and the fee for his time. It's his way of staying free. As I said, he has rules."

"And Kathie?"

I shrugged, and my jacket slipped off my shoulders. Susan helped me slip it back on. "Dixon got her released and we never saw her. She never went back to the rented house. I haven't seen her since."

"I think you were wrong to let her go. She's not someone who should be walking around loose."

"You're probably right," I said. "But she got to be one of us. I couldn't be the one to put her away. When you come down to it, Hawk shouldn't be running loose either."

"I suppose not. So how do you decide?"

I started to shrug again, remembered my jacket, and stopped. "Sometimes I guess, sometimes I trust my instincts, sometimes I don't care. I do what I can."

She smiled. "Yes, you do," she said. "I noticed that at the hotel while I was trying to shower. Even with one arm."

"I'm very powerful," I said.

"A lot of people died this trip out," she said.

"Yes."

"That bothers you some."

"Yes."

"This time worse than many."

"There was a lot of blood. Too much," I said. "People die. Some people probably ought to. But this time there was a lot. I needed to get rid of it. I needed to get clean."

"The fight with Zachary," she said.

"Goddamn," I said. "You don't miss anything, do you?"

"I don't miss very much about you," she said. "I love you. I have come to know you very well."

"Yeah, the fight with Zachary. That was a kind of—what—sweating out the poison, maybe. I don't know. For Hawk too, I think. Or maybe for Hawk it was just competition. He doesn't like to lose. He's not used to it."

"I understand that," she said. "I begin to wonder about myself sometimes. But I understand what you mean."

"Do you understand that there's more?"

"What?"

"You," I said. "The shower assault. It's like I need to love you to come back whole from where I sometimes go."

She rubbed the back of her left hand on my right cheek. "Yes," she said, "I know that too."

The cab pulled up at the Post Office Tower. I paid and

overtipped. We held hands going up in the elevator. It was early evening on a week night. We were seated promptly.

"Touristy," Susan murmured to me. "Very touristy."

"Yes," I said, "but you can have Mateus Rosé and I can have Amstel beer and we can watch the evening settle onto London. We can eat duckling with cherries and I can quote Yeats."

"And later," she said, "there's always another shower."

"Unless I drink too much Amstel," I said, "and eat too much duck with cherries."

"In which likelihood," Susan said, "we can shower in the morning."

Here's a glimpse of Spenser's next adventure. You'll want to read all of LOOKING FOR RACHEL WALLACE, available from Dell.

Spenser may be in over his head
Looking for Rachel Wallace

In front of Manfred's apartment four men were sitting in a two-tone blue Pontiac Bonneville. One of them rolled down the window and yelled across the street, "Your name Spenser?"

"Yeah," I said, "S-p-e-n-s-e-r, like the English poet."

"We want to talk with you," he said.

"Jesus," I said, "I wish I'd thought of saying that."

They piled out of the car. The guy that talked was tall and full of sharp corners, like he'd been assembled from Lego blocks. He had on a navy watch cap and a plaid lumberman's jacket and brown pants that didn't get to the tops of his black shoes. His coat sleeves were too short and his knobby wrists stuck out. His hands were very large with angular knuckles. His jaw moved steadily on something, and as he crossed the street he spat tobacco juice.

The other three were all heavy and looked like men who'd done heavy labor for a long time. The shortest of them had slightly bowed legs, and there was scar tissue thick around his eyes. His nose was thicker than it should have been. I had some of those symptoms myself, and I knew where he got them. Either he hadn't quit as soon as I had or he'd lost more fights. His face looked like a catcher's mitt.

The four of them gathered in front of me on the mall. "What are you doing around here?" the tall one said.

"I'm taking a species count on maggots," I said. "With you four and Manfred I got five right off."

The bow-legged pug said, "He's a smart guy, George. Lemme straighten him out."

George shook his head. He said to me, "You're looking for trouble, you're going to get it. We don't want you bothering Manfred."

"You in the Klan, too?" I said.

"We ain't here to talk, pal," George said.

"You must be in the Klan," I said. "You're a smooth talker and a slick dresser. Where's Manfred—his mom won't let him come out?"

The pug put his right hand flat on my chest and shoved me about two steps backwards. "Get out of here or we'll stomp the shit out of you," he said. He was slow. I hit him two left jabs and a right hook before he even got his hands up. He sat down in the snow.

"No wonder your face got marked up so bad," I said to him. "You got no reflexes."

There was a small smear of blood at the base of the pug's nostrils. He wiped the back of his hand across and climbed to his feet.

"You gonna get it now," he said.

George made a grab at me, and I hit him in the throat. He rocked back. The other two jumped, and the three of us went down in the snow. Someone hit me on the side of the head. I got the heel of my hand under someone's nose and rammed upward. The owner of the nose cried out in pain. George kicked me in the ribs with his steel-toed work shoes. I rolled away, stuck my fingers in someone's eyes, and rolled up onto my feet. The pug hit me a good combination as I was moving past. If I'd been moving toward him, it would have put me down. One of them jumped on my back. I reached up, got hold of his hair, doubled over, and pulled with his momentum. He went over my shoulder and landed on his back on a park bench. The pug hit me on the side of the jaw and I stumbled. He hit me again, and I rolled away from it and lunged against George. He wrapped his arms around me and tried to hold me. I brought both fists up to the level of his ears and pounded them together with his head in between. He grunted and his grip relaxed. I broke free of him and someone hit me with something larger than a fist and the inside of my head got loud and red and I went down.

When I opened my eyes there were granules of snow on the lashes; they looked like magnified salt crystals. There was no sound and no movement. Then there was a snuffing sound. I rolled my eyes to the left, and over the small rim of snow I could see a black nose with slight pink outlinings. It snuffed at me. I shifted my head slightly and said, *"Uff."* The nose pulled back. It was on one end of a dog, an apprehensive young Dalmatian that stood with its front legs stiffened and its hindquarters raised and its tail making uncertain wags.

Lifting my head was too hard. I put it back in the snow. The dog moved closer and snuffed at me again. I heard someone yell, "Digger!" The dog shuffled his feet uncertainly.

Someone yelled "Digger!" again, and the dog moved away. I took a deep breath. It hurt my ribcage. I exhaled, inhaled again, inched my arms under me, and pushed myself up onto my hands and knees. My head swam. I felt my stomach tighten, and I threw up, which hurt the ribs some more. I stayed that way for a bit, on my hands and knees with my head hanging, like a winded horse. My eyes focused a little better. I could see the snow and the dog's footprints, beyond them the legs of a park bench. I crawled over, got hold of it, and slowly got myself upright. Everything blurred for a minute, then came back into focus again. I inhaled some more and felt a little steadier. I looked around. The mall was empty. The Dalmatian was a long way down the mall now, walking with a man and woman. The snow where I stood was trampled and churned. There was a lot of blood spattered on the snow. Across the street in front of Manfred's apartment the Pontiac was gone. I felt my mouth with my left hand. It was swollen, but no teeth were loose. My nose seemed okay, too.

I let go of the bench and took a step. My ribs were stiff and sore. My head ached. I had to wait for a moment while dizziness came and went. I touched the back of my head. It was swollen and wet with blood. I took a handful of snow from the bench seat and held it against the swollen part. Then I took another step, and another. I was under way. My apartment was three blocks away—one block to Marlborough Street, two blocks down toward the Public Garden. I figured I'd make it by sundown.